USA TODAY BESTSELLING AUTHOR

DALE MAYER

contemporary romance

SCALES

BROKEN BUT... MENDING #3

SCALES (OF JUSTICE)
Beverly Dale Mayer
Valley Publishing Ltd.

Copyright © 2015

This is a work of fiction. Names, characters, places, brands, media, and incidents are either the product of the author's imagination or are used fictitiously. Any resemblance to actual events, locales, or persons, living or dead, is entirely coincidental.

ISBN-13: 978-1-988315-89-8
Print Edition

About This Book

What can balance the scales of justice when hearts are shattered, pain is inflicted and damage is dealt beyond repair?

Paris escaped a situation that some would consider a crime. She worries constantly that the day of reckoning is coming for her around every corner. Weaver seeks justice with the avidity of a hunter seeking prey. His biggest fear is that the day of reckoning he deserves will never come.

Forced to deal with very deep and individual problems, Paris and Weaver – strangers who are complete opposites – agree to a therapy assignment that includes only the two of them and that initially seems radical and a little scary.

Against shattered hearts, inflicted pain and irreparable damage, can love balance the scales of justice?

Sign up to be notified of all Dale's releases here!
https://geni.us/DaleNews

CHAPTER 1

PARIS WILSON SAT with her back to the wall and waited as the room slowly filled up for the first morning seminar. They'd all briefly met the night before but the real workshop started today. Set in downtown Vancouver, at a posh but business-style hotel, she couldn't help but feel this Inner Healing workshop could be the answer to so many problems. It had better be, especially after pleading with her professor that she was ready for this. It was a special workshop for university students under Professor Jenna Komak. And Jenna alone made the decision as to who would be allowed to attend.

Now Paris was here and couldn't wait to get started. She had picked a perfect spot to watch the other attendees but only be seen by a few of them as they looked around. Those she could ignore.

She'd ignore everyone if she could. They were a distraction. There was a reason she was here and she was anxious to get started. Several reasons actually. When her brother, Sean, had attended the same workshop earlier this summer, he'd fallen in love with a special woman he'd met there. Robin was stunning inside and out.

Paris was seriously happy for Sean. She'd always known he'd find someone someday – even if he hadn't believed it. Not only because he was her brother, but because he was a great man and a terrific human being.

He deserved to be happy. And that made all the difference in the world.

Brushing back her black hair, Paris knew that any of these other attendees could potentially impact her life in a similar way. In wonder, she studied the few people taking seats at the very front. She'd never been able to do that. Being front and center. It put too much attention on her. Considering how eager she was to get moving on this, she should probably consider the risks. Even though her hopes were high for the workshop, she knew she was asking a lot. She was eager. Too eager. She didn't have rose-colored glasses with which to view the world, but she had her brother's experience as a standard.

Dropping her gaze to her hands, her fingers picked away at the skin from the base of the nails. Ugly. Damaged. Falling to pieces. Gee funny, her outside matched her inside.

At that, she almost gave an audible snort but held it back at the last moment. It wouldn't do to attract attention in this setting. She settled back and watched as several men took their seats. The only men she knew well had been her father and her brother. Both of them were so much alike and so opposite in all the ways that counted. Other males she met seemed to be a mix of the two. Maybe that was good. Maybe not.

She'd been interested in a few men she'd met through work, but knew they wouldn't want her. What was to want? She was an okay size as in shorter than Sean but just a hair taller than his partner Robin. Even though she ate like a horse, she was slim, bordering on gaunt. Her brother said she was too nervy to keep any weight on. Whatever.

She had to admit to being a little on the driven Type A

side, but she had a reason. After missing out on so much in life, she couldn't help but want to do more. Be more.

Then there was the mixed-up part of her that knew she could never be enough. Never be good enough. She hadn't ever been *that* good. And that perception impacted her actions every day.

It was stupid. She was an adult now. Surely her childhood shouldn't be doing this to her anymore.

Except, whispered that gentle voice inside, *you weren't a child when it finally stopped. You were a teenager. So very vulnerable to the actions, opinions of those around you. Very impressionable at an age where you'd already been beaten into the ground. Knew there was no one out there that would save you. Already understood that the original fairy tales had the right of it, they were grim, heart-wrenching stories. Nothing like the pretty pink stories she heard other kids talk about with teddy bears and rainbows and unicorns even.*

Paris knew the bogeyman was real. And she knew that there was one inside of every single person – including herself.

"Is anyone sitting here?"

The deep dark voice shook her to the core. Surprised at the swarthy young man standing beside her, she stared uncomprehendingly at him. She glanced at the direction he pointed and realized she'd been sitting in one chair and taking up a second chair with her legs, subconsciously giving people no choice but to stay away. Jenna, their professor, would have a heyday with her body language.

Paris dropped her legs and muttered, "No, it's free."

Nodding, he sat down, turning his back to her.

She studied him covertly. As broad as Sean was lean, he was solid looking. Farmer stock. Big hands and forearms but not the muscle-bound body builder type. Nice actually.

And there was a faint smell, not cologne, subtler than that. Aftershave or even shaving soap. With his dark coloring, she imagined he had to shave a couple of times a day. He turned and gave her a bland look.

She flushed. Damn it, he'd caught her studying him.

Back in school, she had learned that if she went into class afraid, the teacher would pick on her to do a question on the board. She always got picked. However, if she walked in and couldn't have cared less about it, she never got picked. *How come she couldn't apply that same trick to the world at large?* Paris wondered.

The instructor walked in at that moment. The air magically twisted, becoming lighter, airy. The underlying nervousness quickly dissipated.

Paris was here for the same thing everyone else was here for. To heal.

They all needed to move past issues that stopped them from leading the fulfilling lives they all wanted. They all wanted to move forward.

Simple. Not.

Jenna had achieved phenomenal results with her earlier seminars, but at what point did her special touch run a little thin? Paris knew if the magic was going to run out, it would run out with her. She hadn't learned the trick of making her life happen easily. Nor of making it through life unscathed like so many people she knew. Neither did she expect much more than what she had.

But she wished…dreamed…fantasized of so much more.

Especially babies.

And there were just some things that no matter how much wishing one did, it wasn't going to happen.

Still, the alternative would have been worse. She was here, and she was strong and healthy and alive. She was good with that. There were alternative dreams she could dream.

She smiled.

And damn if her neighbor didn't turn and looked at her suspiciously.

It was her turn to give him a bland stare.

He cocked one eyebrow, a glint of amusement in his gaze before he shifted back in his chair and turned his attention to the front of the room.

Only she caught sight of a muscle in his jaw twitching in a steady pulsating manner.

Squeezing her eyes shut, she tried to focus on Jenna's words. That's why she was here. Her eyes popped open. Yet at the same time her neighbor, in the chair next to her, was starting to drive her nuts. She wanted to slap a hand over that muscle and make it stop.

Just part of her stress management techniques she had to work on. Fix what she could fix and ignore what she couldn't. So how was she doing on that second half? Lousy.

Jenna held up a stack of folders. "Good morning, everyone."

A murmured response rippled through the room.

"I'm glad to see you've all settled in, we'll work first on getting you divvied up into pairs and then hand out the assignments. Until I call your name, remember I mentioned homework last night? Well this..." She held up a stack of papers to the groans of those around her, "Won't be homework if you get it all done now."

And with that, she dropped the stack at the front desk and said, "Take one and pass them around."

Paris watched as the stack moved from one person to the

other. She'd be last. Maybe that was okay too.

Jenna called two people's names and moved the couple to the back of the room where three chairs sat in a cozy arrangement in the corner. Paris kept half an eye on their reactions but as there were lots of smiles and nods, she figured the first couple wasn't unhappy with their assignment. A few moments later, the couple returned and Jenna called out two more names and asked the attendees to join her at the back.

Somewhere in there, the assignment sheet arrived on the table in front of Paris. She picked it up and sighed. This one was a sheet on dreams. Your dreams. Dreams you gave up on. Dreams you couldn't give up on. And the last one got to Paris – list the innermost secret dream you were too afraid to let yourself dream.

She stared at that question and wished she had an answer.

"For those of you working on the homework sheet," Jenna said. "Please add one question to the bottom of the sheet."

There were long, heavy sighs from those around her.

Paris looked at Jenna, waiting, wondering where she was going with this.

"Write down the biggest regret in your life and how the event impacted your dreams."

Shit.

Paris's hard-won calm disintegrated. That question required no thought.

She already had the answer. She lived with it daily.

She wished she'd never killed her father.

WHAT WAS PARIS'S problem? Cool name. If he'd read the top of worksheet correctly.

But the woman…her expression was that of a deer frozen in the spotlight. He stared at her, seeing the glassy eyes and the stark-white pallor.

Like what the hell?

Trying to sneak a glance at her paper again, he realized she was filling out the question that Jenna had just added. All he could see was something ending with *her father.*

Figures. Every messed-up girl seemed to have daddy issues. While he turned back to his paper, he kept an eye on her. When she started to rub out the words written on her paper – words written in pen – he knew she wasn't all there.

The questions in front of him were beyond his understanding, but he had to ponder the concept. He wasn't about dreams. He was all about goals. Dreams were nebulous. Airy and light. Weightless. Euphemism for useless. He was a planner. A-one-foot-in-front-of-the-other-and-walk toward a specific end point kind of person. Not for the joy of the walk but because he was going to get somewhere specific. He was all about specifics. That he was here in this damn class said he was doing one of the steps that he needed to do to get on with his life.

Another check box was being marked off. Good. Therapy wasn't his thing, especially not his own. At least not now. No, he couldn't really say for sure why he was here except because of Jenna herself. He'd heard about Jenna's classes and had even attended several of her evening lectures. But he didn't *need* her class and he'd told her so. That's when she'd smiled that really witchy smile, her eyes glowing with laughter, and she'd challenged him to attend. To show that he'd taken care of *his* stuff. That there wasn't anything else she could show him.

"Hell," he'd said with a snicker, "of course I *could* do it, but I don't need to. I wouldn't pay good money for something like this."

With a laugh, she replied, "If you think you're immune, then write up a paper on it. If it's any good, I'll help you get it published. If you find out you're not immune, we'll revisit the subject of the report at the end."

Now that appealed to his sense of purpose. His portfolio was missing published articles – particularly in peer-reviewed journals. Even if having a shrink's name on his paper didn't help in getting a paper published, it was on his bucket list. And damn it, that bucket list was important.

So he'd accepted the challenge. And here he was.

So no, he hadn't been tricked into attending, but…it almost felt like it. Or maybe it was that he felt played…and had taken the bait. And that now he was where she wanted him to be.

But why?

To observe? To write his insights? There was lots of fodder here. Some of these people needed serious help.

He shook his head and scratched the word dreams out and replaced it with the word goals. When he was done, he realized the odd sound beside him was the sound of paper ripping. He snuck a glance over at Paris to see her trying to rip out the answer she'd tried to rub out first. Apparently, she was seriously determined to not let anyone see that answer. As he studied her, he realized that she'd actually ripped off the strip of paper and had rolled it up into a tiny ball.

Fascinated, he watched her struggle to find a place to hide the tiny item. He couldn't take his eyes off it. What the hell had she written that she wanted erased so badly?

His gaze swung back to the paper. She'd left the other answers intact. Just a long strip missing out of the bottom half. As if sensing his bewilderment, she lifted her gaze to his face. Her cheeks flared with bright colors as their eyes met, and she slammed her hand over the same hand that held the tiny ball of paper. The ball flew from her fingers, bounced on the table, and rolled toward him.

It was inevitable. The curious behavior he witnessed had him itching to know what she was trying to hide; what was written on the crumpled ball on the floor in front of him. Just as he reached for the paper ball, she snatched it up, their fingers brushing briefly as he watched the trail of her fingers to her mouth.

She popped the tiny globe into her mouth…and damn if she didn't swallow it.

CHAPTER 2

P ARIS SHUDDERED WITH embarrassment. Oh God. Oh Lord. Please say she hadn't just done that.

She'd been so panicked when she'd seen him first glance at her paper. The answer she had written. An answer she'd never intended to share. There'd never been any consideration that someone else would read it. Of course Jenna. But then she already knew.

The thought of anyone else knowing…she struggled to control her breathing. Closing her eyes, she took one deep breath, then a second one. It was impossible to have a panic attack here, she didn't dare. She hadn't had one in a long time…

A shadow fell across her face. A heavy hand landed on her shoulder. "Are you okay?" asked a deep rolling male voice.

Opening her eyes in a flash, she knew before she saw that it was him.

Her gaze widened and she swallowed. Finally, she managed to nod and whisper, "Yes, thank you."

Hard eyes stared down at her, studying her. As though he was looking into the very heart of her. Quickly, her eyes slammed closed before he could see too much.

See the guilty stain on her soul. Sense the vast emptiness inside.

"Hey, take it easy."

The fingers on her shoulders squeezed gently. The warmth of his touch pulsed through her and she took another breath.

"Okay," she said, nodding as she opened her eyes and gave him a lopsided grin. "Believe it or not, I'm trying to."

"Try harder." That tone said *do it*. No excuses. And something about it worked. She straightened up, gave him a small nod of thanks, and glanced down at her paper. The paper was destroyed, ripped to shreds. "Wow, I really didn't like that question."

Her neighbor barked with laughter.

"Or you liked it so well, you had to taste it," he teased.

Without any malice or jeering in his tone, she took no offense. "A hang-up from my childhood," she admitted.

"Good thing the rest of the questions are fine then," he said, startling a laugh out of her.

"Paris and Weaver."

They both turned to face Jenna standing beside them.

"Sorry," Paris rushed to say, "I wasn't paying attention."

Jenna's sharp eyes landed on Paris's face. Her mouth opened as if to say something but she held back. Then she switched her gaze to Weaver and gave him a small nod.

And it was that nod that Paris really wanted to understand.

Because it was a small satisfied nod, as if she was happy with a decision he'd made. And what decision that was, Paris couldn't begin to fathom. Still, Jenna's arrival was enough to help Paris rebalance and get back on track.

Then Jenna's gaze widened as she stared at something on the table. Paris groaned silently. Her damn worksheet. Shoulders slumped, she opened her mouth to explain when

Jenna said, "If you two could come to the back with me now, please."

And she turned and walked away.

Paris was confused for a moment, but she got up, reached for her paper, and realized it was gone.

As she spun around searching for it, she saw Weaver, and what a different name that was, hold out a small square of paper.

Stretching her hand out to accept it, she suddenly realized it was her worksheet now folded so the rips didn't show – into a perfect little star.

She laughed. "Thanks."

"No problem." He motioned behind her. "Let's go. Jenna is waiting."

HE WAITED FOR her to stumble to her feet and race to the back of the room. To get away from him? Or to get to Jenna faster? If so, she was the only one. All the other attendees had dragged their feet.

In his mind, he was taking notes on her character. While doing his masters in psychology, he'd learned, seen many interesting people, and heard fascinating cases. All of the bits and pieces of various personalities that made them the whole of who they were. Through these cases, he began to understand how events in life disintegrated the calm exterior of some and shattered the interior of others. Coping skills were as wide and varied as the people and the catastrophic event in their lives were.

Though he'd studied cases, attended cases as an observer, and had read widely, he'd yet to touch the tip of what made people tick. Jenna had a special touch. Partly why he'd attended so many lectures. To try and understand how she'd achieved the results she had from her workshops.

He wasn't sure what he was going to do with his degree. Something useful he hoped. But he couldn't do what Jenna did, and neither could he work in the hospitals where so many people needed help. He wasn't at the point of helping others yet.

Maybe down the road that could be an option but, he knew how quickly his own buttons could get pushed. Even after years of working on his own crap. There was a buffer layer between the buttons and reality, but somehow being at the hospital, working with patients, and dealing with major psychological issues made that cushion thin like nothing else. He always felt exposed when he was there. As if he wore a sign that made it clear he was exactly the same as they were. That they shouldn't look to him for help.

It crossed his mind that most people finishing their degrees felt ineffective in facing the world, afraid the world might expect them to have answers now that the initial stages of schooling were complete.

That's one thing he did know – he was short on answers. "Weaver?"

Startled, he looked over at Jenna, who was waiting for him. When she motioned to the seat beside him, he realized he'd stopped beside the two women and had stood lost in thought while they waited for him to sit.

What an idiot. With an apologetic smile, he sat.

"Now that you are both here…" she waited and gave Weaver a brief smile, "I wanted to go over the project you'll both take part in." He started. No, that hadn't been part of the deal. Already having agreed to write, a paper, he didn't want to have to take part in the week-long activity. How was he going to find time to do both?

Yeah, he wasn't. So Paris could do the project while he did his paper. Sounded fair to him, but somehow he didn't think it would be that easy.

"Normally I assign a specific challenge to a two-person team…" She broke off and shuffled papers on her desk. "In your case, Paris, you have specific issues that you need to resolve, and I may have a way forward for you. In Weaver's case, he's dealing with the opposite side of the same coin, in a more minor way."

Weaver looked at Jenna then switched to see an odd expression whisper across Paris's face.

Cautiously, Weaver asked, "And what coin is that, exactly?"

A knowing smile in her gaze startled him as much as her answer. She said, "Justice."

CHAPTER 3

JUSTICE?

Paris couldn't stop the shaking that threatened to overtake her body. Was there ever a word that scared her more? The police had cleared her, she had not been charged. In fact, she'd been praised for her quick actions, her quick thinking. For saving her brother. But somehow inside she knew she was going to pay for what she'd done. It was a dark shadow that hung over her – all the time. Waiting for someone to know a miscarriage of justice had been done and finally take her into custody.

The thoughts, the fears, overtook everything. It was almost more than she could bear. No amount of reassurance from the police, social workers, or any of the numerous therapists she'd gone to removed the fear – she knew the truth. She was guilty.

One day the specter in her life – Justice – was going to prevail.

And then there was Constable Barry Delaney. His words – his warning. Something she'd never forget.

"Justice is easy," Weaver said, snapping her back to the present as he quoted. "There are no two sides to that coin. Black is black and white is white. Right and wrong are easy to sort out."

Paris glanced over at him, still shaken by the conversation. Could he really be so naïve? Was anything in life that cut and dried?

"You're spouting lecture notes of our esteemed Professor Marshal Henniker, I presume," Jenna said with a laugh.

"You don't believe him," Weaver challenged, a glint in his eye.

"I know Henniker actively incites debates in his lectures, but he doesn't believe it either. However, as a teaching tool, it is effective in gaining student participation."

"I can imagine," Paris muttered under her breath. At the sharp look from Weaver, she pinched her lips together and stared back.

"You don't believe in Justice?" he asked mockingly.

"Of course," she said smoothly. "However, there are definite shades of gray in that argument."

He gave a half snort. "Whatever."

Jenna grinned. "So now you two can work out your project." She stood.

"Wait, what?" Paris asked. "What project? You haven't said anything about what we're supposed to do." The panicky part of her that was screaming for detailed instructions was something she hated. Steps to follow, so she wouldn't stray off the path or wander aimlessly and get nothing done. It wasn't that she needed to be micromanaged, but she did need to know what was required of her.

The thought of not knowing made her sick to her stomach. Things needed to be laid out in front of her. Expectations clearly defined. So she didn't do it wrong. So she didn't end up in trouble.

So she didn't fail.

"You'll figure it out," Jenna said cheerfully.

"No, wait," Paris said, a hint of panic in her voice. "We

don't know anything about what the project is supposed to accomplish. Why do we need to do a project in the first place?" she asked in what she hoped was a reasonable tone. Inside, her stomach twisted. There needed to be more direction, more to work with here. Didn't Jenna see that?

Jenna sat down again, studying Paris's face intently.

Paris flinched. Damn it.

"You're here to heal. You're here to grow past an issue that is impeding your growth. You're here to leave it behind and move forward as the strong, capable, caring woman you truly are." Then she smiled that beautiful smile that was like a radiant hug and added, "So a project where you actively work on this issue is the best way forward. It doesn't have to be about Justice, but it should be related."

And she got up, turned, and added, "Oh, and there is no right or wrong way to do this. In other words, you can't fail." With another beautiful smile, she left.

Paris watched her leave before glancing around the room. Everyone had someone. They were all talking in pairs, discussing their projects, their plans.

She was lost. Adrift, when she needed an anchor.

Weaver shifted in his chair until he was directly in front of her view, effectively blocking out the others. "So what would you like to do?"

Her gaze widened. How had she forgotten she wasn't alone? Weaver was her partner for this project. Instantly she felt better. "I have no idea."

"About justice. And it's to help you grow past your issues."

"My issues?" For some reason, that superior tone of voice maybe, his comment made her back bristle. "What about *your* issues?"

He opened his mouth, then thought better of it and slumped back into his chair.

"Yeah, I thought so." She glared at him.

"She said we were on opposite sides of the coin and we supposedly both have some work to do in that area, so really given what little she said, we need to find a way back to the middle instead of being on one side or the other," he said thoughtfully. "Not that it's an easy thing to do. How about how Justice has transformed our lives?"

Instead of answering him, she studied his face as he pondered the issue. Why was he here? Everyone in Jenna's classes were the same as she was, in need and broken in some way. Weaver looked out of place. Like he should be the lecturer, not the attendee. As if he had nothing to get over. Nothing to gain from being here. Except everyone did.

Even him.

She smiled. He just didn't know it yet.

WHAT WAS HER problem? Weaver tried to watch unobtrusively as Paris's lips twitched. As if she knew something he didn't. He narrowed his gaze at her.

As she looked around and then glanced back at him, he stood and watched her. Everything about her made her appear lost. Well, he for one was damn hungry. They'd been last or second to last in terms of getting their assignment and as assignments went, it was a complete dud. He should know, he'd just completed years of them. "Let's have lunch and discuss our options."

"Options?" she asked cautiously.

He wanted to smile but wasn't sure what her caution stemmed from and didn't want her to think he was making fun of her. Stepping aside, he motioned her to go ahead of him out of the lecture room. The other participants were collecting their belongings and starting to meander in the direction of the doorway. If they got to the restaurant first, he'd have a decent chance of being served faster.

"Options for the project."

"Oh." And damn if her footsteps didn't slow. With a gentle hand at her lower back, he nudged her forward slightly. "Let's grab a table while we still can. The group is coming behind us."

His steady touch propelled her forward to the hallway. He'd intended to remove his hand from her long lean back as soon as they were moving in the right direction, but something held his hand where it was, gently stroking the long lean muscles on the side of her spine. He desperately wanted to stretch out his fingers and explore the long ribs so tantalizingly close or drift around and see if his eyesight was as good as he thought it was at measuring her tiny waist. She had a yoga body and appeared muscled and fit. On one hand he yearned to know more about her, but at the same time knew her story would tug at his heartstrings and was better left alone.

He didn't do heartstrings.

He'd seen so much pain, death, and anguish, he knew he was better off alone, at least for now.

That way his buttons couldn't get pushed.

He also knew Jenna would have fun with him on her shrink couch. Sure, he'd come a long way, but that didn't mean there wasn't room for him to still travel down that road back to normal.

Yet, he'd come far enough to feel comfortable in his own skin. And comfortable enough that he didn't want to change that state again. Change hurt.

The frailty of the human condition was something he understood well.

And he didn't want to crash and burn. Rebuilding was hard. It took a long time. He had a lot of respect for those working on their own issues. But he'd made it to a point of not having to do more. It was possible to stop here at this stage if he wanted to. He'd done enough. He was good now.

Resetting his attention on Paris, he noticed her wispy long hair and super clean nails with the ragged edges. Her fingernails had ragged edges. He wondered at the familiarity he now recognized, the general look to her. Then he knew. It shouldn't have taken him so long. After all, he'd met many of them.

"You're a nurse."

She spun. "What?" Her voice squeaked out just the one shocked word.

His eyebrows shot up. Interesting response.

"I'm sorry; I didn't mean to get personal. It just occurred to me that you look like a nurse."

Her eyes darkened as she stared at him, taking a step back. They'd been hazel, but damn if they didn't look green now. She muttered something under her breath and turned away, almost racing toward the restaurant now.

Skittish, like a colt, he thought to himself, content to follow at a slower pace, wondering at the woman in front of him. She was an enigma.

And he was fascinated.

CHAPTER 4

W HAT THE HELL was wrong with her? Weaver was just another man. She worked with dozens of them. Most were decent, hardworking, take-their-paychecks-home-to-the-family kind of guys. There were a few players. Nurses were notorious for getting hit upon. It had been a joke in college with the engineers. As if they were a natural pairing. The guys had certainly believed it. As nurses had been generally pretty, compassionate, and nice people, they'd always been popular. If you knew one nurse and invited her to a party, then everyone hoped she'd bring her fellow students.

Paris got along with all the men at work, but she never got involved with any. She loved her job and would never do anything to jeopardize it. Her focus at work was babies. Mothers and babies. But mostly babies. Even being here for the week was pulling at her, making her worried about the patients she'd left behind. She trusted her coworkers; they were a brilliant team of specialists and cared about the patients as much as she did.

But nothing compared to the joy of the babies them-selves. She adored them and wanted a half dozen but knew realistically two or three were more reasonable. Even if she couldn't have them herself. There were many babies out there needing someone to love them. And love was something she had in abundance. When the time was right, she would adopt.

Right now, though, she wasn't ready.

That was partly why she was here.

To become ready. To deal with her failures. Her belief she didn't deserve more. To deal with her lacks. Come to terms with the things in her life she could never have. Never experience. Adjust to her situation. To the injustice of it.

And damn, that brought her back around to Jenna and her words. Something she had said about her and Weaver being on the opposite sides of Justice. How did that work? In her head, Paris knew right and wrong was a gray area. It depended entirely on the situation. She had to believe that or else she would have turned herself in. And of course that was the problem – she couldn't believe that theory one hundred percent – but she wanted to. She was always looking over her shoulder, afraid that a mistake had been made in the system and the police were coming after her now. She wanted to be free of that fear.

"How about over there?"

Pulled back to the present, Paris glanced over at the window seat that Weaver had pointed out. "That's fine," she muttered. It was actually better than fine – it looked cozy, intimate in a way. This immediately brought to mind the heat of Weaver's hand on her back earlier as he'd guided her here. She shoved the thought deep inside and focused on her surroundings. The hotel restaurant was busy and didn't look to be horribly expensive. It also catered to downtown businesses and should offer a decent selection of food.

Not that she was very hungry.

He led the way and took the seat furthest away. She slipped into the closest one.

With a lift of a hand, the waitress came over immediately. As soon as she arrived, he ordered a double burger, fries, and coffee. When the waitress turned to Paris, she shrugged. "I don't even know what you have here."

The waitress rattled off the daily special and snagged a menu off a neighboring table. Except when she reached for the menu, the waitress mentioned fish and chips. Paris dropped the menu and said, "I'll have that, thanks."

After deciding on one or two pieces, and coleslaw and the fries, the waitress grabbed the menu. "I'll be back in a few minutes with coffee," she said, then hurried away.

"Have you eaten here before?" Paris asked. "You seemed to know what to order."

"I had breakfast here."

"Oh." That explained it. Paris hadn't slept well and had missed breakfast. She'd slipped into the lecture room with a take-out coffee and nothing else. At least she hadn't had a sugary cookie with it. But she'd been tempted.

Fish and chips weren't the healthiest of choices either, but she was really hungry and stressed and the afternoon was likely to be worse.

"So how do you see this report working?" she asked. "I'm used to being given a few more parameters than this."

"Partly why Jenna didn't give them to us." He shrugged. "She also knows I'm in grad school, and we often have to come up with a thesis statement and write a report about it."

Paris sat in quiet contemplation for a moment. "And what are you envisioning with this report then?" And how the hell was it going to help her? She dropped her gaze to the table, her finger aimlessly tracing the diagonal pattern in the tabletop.

"If you tell me why you're so stuck on the one side of

justice or how it has helped or hindered your transformation, then I'll tell you mine. Our journey from here could be the report."

Paris sat back against the vinyl bench seat and stared. "And what if that journey is beyond us to make?"

"The journey is the issue, not the end result. As long as we make the attempt, then that is the report."

Holding back a sneer, she replied, "You don't seem to feel you have any traveling to do on that pathway."

He studied her, a surprised look in his gaze. "What makes you say that?"

"Your complete detachment at the concept. It doesn't make you afraid or worried in any way at the thought of doing something like this."

Instead of answering, he shifted his cutlery around in front of him.

And she watched, understanding she'd hit a nerve. "We all have something to learn," she said gently. "Even when we don't think we do."

Lifting his head, his eyes shone. "I'm not saying I don't have anything to learn. I'm just not sure I have anything to learn in this area…"

"Ah. Interesting."

The waitress arrived, cutting off further speech. Paris watched as he attacked his plate of food with more enthusiasm than necessary. It said much about his state of mind. She smiled and lifted a fry. "See, you do have much to learn in this area."

He froze, his burger mid air, his gaze dark, defensive. "What I might have to learn doesn't mean I'm ready or able or indeed willing to do so here."

"Ditto."

There was a moment of silence as he chewed and swallowed his food. "So tell me what you think about Justice. And then tell me what you'd like your stance to be."

How about the fact that she hated the topic? That she hated the concept of there being two sides to the issue. Since when was anything so clear-cut, so black and white. Figures that Jenna would pick up on it. Anything that made Paris feel so strongly was something to explore when it came to therapy. She stared out the window, wondering what to answer.

"I am not sure I have a stance on it, actually. I think the circumstances often determine my view."

"Explain."

She shrugged. "I'm not pro-abortion, but if the mother was raped, I could easily understand her not wanting the child."

"Except it's not the child's fault, and it has the right to life."

"Exactly what I mean." Now they were getting somewhere. "There are a lot of debates and understanding required for either side. Gray areas."

He frowned and continued to eat. "Or do you have a specific stance, but on a specific issue."

Stopping suddenly, she could feel the flags of heat burn through her cheeks. "Maybe. And maybe not," she snapped. "What about you? What are you so decided on that Jenna thinks you need to learn something different?"

He laughed. "Jenna doesn't know anything about me." Then he shut up.

"Did you attend her lectures? Her evening classes?" At his nod, she asked, "Have a special meeting with her about this seminar?"

He nodded again.

A smile spread across her face and she sat back. "Then regardless of what you think she might or might not know about you, I can tell you she understands more than you think."

Did he see that? She looked for a glimmer of understanding, but when there was only a hooded glance her way, she wasn't sure she'd gotten through to him. And that damn tiny knowing smile that played at the corner of his lips. What was with that?

"You think I'm wrong, don't you?"

"Not at all." He shook his head. "But my situation is different from yours, so my discussion with Jenna would have been slightly different than yours would have been."

Paris held back her smile. She understood. He thought he was different. Thought he didn't have the same problems the other participants had. Well, she didn't have that problem, but her brother sure had. At least until he'd been through one of these seminars.

Weaver, she suspected, would be the same.

"What are you doing at the university?"

He dropped his gaze to the table then hesitated, as if undecided as to what to say. Fair enough, she thought as she absentmindedly took another fry and bit off half of it.

"I'm completing my masters in psychology."

Oh shit. That couldn't be good. Then he really did it.

"Jenna was one of my Profs last year," he said calmly. "I'm going to write a report on her workshop. She says if it's any good, she'll help me get it published."

Paris dropped the rest of her french fry on her plate. Shocked, she said, "You mean this workshop is a school assignment? I'm supposed to be part of some damn study so you can get a professional checkmark?" Now that was too much. Blinking back the sudden moisture in the corner of her eyes, she got up from her chair and walked unsteadily out of the restaurant. Out of the hotel. Too bad she couldn't walk out of the damn workshop.

HE SHOULDN'T HAVE told her. He'd made a monumental mistake. Why? He knew better. But she'd gotten too close. He'd gotten defensive. Not wanting to believe her. He gazed out the window, deep in thought. The one time he needed to keep his big mouth shut. He cursed under his breath. Of course he knew better. This was a report. A study. One never told the subjects when they were involved, if they needed to give natural responses. Once they had the information of belonging to a study group, they acted differently from a different set of parameters.

Still, she might *not* be in his report. He hadn't figured out how to target the report yet. And he'd never use names.

Given the little bit he'd seen of Paris, he didn't think she knew what a parameter was. She appeared to be a ball of insecurity masquerading as something with poise and confidence and failing entirely. Like a five-year-old girl using mommy's makeup and parading through the house trying to look grown up. Instead, she looked exactly like a little girl who was trying too hard.

Paris was definitely trying too hard.

Still, he'd done something horribly wrong. As he stared out the window, oblivious to the scene on the outside of the glass, he realized there was no help for it. The next step was to go to Jenna and confess.

Crap.

He hated being in the wrong. Hated apologizing. It always made him feel lousy. Something he never quite got over.

He learned from a young age that being wrong meant a good beating. Even now, he had to talk to the adult side of his nature and explain that getting your ass kicked for being wrong was a long time ago. This is what life is all about now. Deal with it.

CHAPTER 5

"I WANT A new partner," Paris said baldly from the open doorway. If she hadn't been staring at Jenna so closely, she might have missed seeing the slight headshake before it firmed up.

Jenna lifted her head and gave Paris the sweetest smile.

"No." Paris entered the room and plunked down on a chair beside her. "No excuses or platitudes about why this pairing is a good idea or anything else. I am no one's assignment," she cried out, her voice rising. Then anger bloomed. "And no way am I going into a damn report about my experiences this week."

A cloud briefly dimmed the joy in Jenna's face. "I'm not surprised you feel that way," she said gently. "I would too."

That made Paris pause. "Then why me?" she asked, her hands curling into fists. "Why would you pair him up with me?"

"Because he needs you," Jenna said, compassion and understanding in her voice. "And you need him."

"No way." Paris shook her head, her long black hair flying everywhere. "I need understanding and tolerance. Patience. Someone to show me the way. To help me take the steps I need to take." She glared at Jenna. "I don't need someone who considers himself my superior in all ways. Who thinks he can analyze what makes me tick. Who thinks he knows what's best for me."

As Jenna opened her mouth to answer, Paris rolled right over her. "The only person who can know that, the only one who understands my life to that depth to make those types of answers, is me."

She stood. "I won't have it. I won't be in his damn report."

And she hurried to the door.

"What if I told you," Jenna called after her, "that writing that report was his lesson?"

Paris hit the brakes at the doorway. "What do you mean?"

"Everyone is here to learn. Everyone here has some major roadblock in their life that they need to move past. How they move past is just as important as making sure that they do get past it. Weaver needs to write this all down. He needs to put it into orderly form. It's all about control. Detaching from his own world, that he might understand how other people are learning to help themselves."

"And what will that give him? Except boost his satisfaction of being better than everyone?" Paris asked in a hard voice. "It makes it very hard to like him, you know."

Jenna smiled a breathtaking smile, as if she'd come to some major realization.

"Of course it does. So why do you think he does it?"

"So no one will like him," Paris joked. Then as Jenna nodded slowly, she walked across the floor to stand in front of her. "He doesn't think he's likable, right?"

That smile rose brighter.

"He figures no one will love him anyway, doesn't he?" And Paris understood. "So he's going to push them away before he gets pushed away."

She collapsed on her chair. "Damn."

HE WAS FILLED with regrets. *What are you going to do about it, idiot? Apologize? Tell Jenna you won't do the report as you've messed this up already. And just what is she likely to say?* Weaver pondered the issue as he paid the bill and wandered out to the lobby. She'd smile and tell him to fix it.

How the hell could he do that?

Really, all he wanted was to get this report published. In a way, he needed the credits. They could be damn hard to get. He wanted to move forward into his field and help people. He understood he might not be ready, but no one said he had to go full bore into this. A little at a time – at a rate he could handle. That worked.

So what if he lost a little skin scraping close to his issues or gained another scar or two? More scars would just add to the many he already had. But then, Paris had scars of her own, he'd seen some of them. And even he could feel the open wound he'd caused.

"So apologize," he said out loud. "That's the place to start."

Glancing down at his watch, he realized he had a little time before the afternoon lecture started. Good. He could get a start and write down his impressions. The things he'd picked up already. And there were a lot.

The seminar room was empty when he arrived. He took his seat and opened his laptop to take a look at the report he'd set up but hadn't done much with yet. Now he let his mind go and let his fingers fly on the keyboard as he wrote down a description of Paris. It was her that interested him.

Confused, valiant, emotional. Damaged. Obviously

hurt, but tired of hurting. There is strength in her, but she has never been strong enough to deal with the core hurt. She's alive, but a part of her is dead.

He stopped and read what he'd written. Wow. So much for analytical. This was literally emotional, the impressions from his gut. Though there was no way to verify if he was right or wrong, his mind and heart said he was on track. Paris was an eager beaver desperate to get over something and get on with the next stage of her life, and that concept both terrified and excited her. Failure was not an option, yet he suspected it was quite likely the outcome. Not that he'd wished that for her, but she was a mass of confusion even for herself.

Then there was the damn project. How did that work if there were no outlines to follow? No theme to grab onto. No guidelines. He highly suspected it was Jenna's way of making them think. But that didn't mean Paris would get the outcome she hoped for. The outcome she needed from it.

So what could he do to help it become reality?

He owed her after all. And he wanted her to be okay with this report.

So he'd need her to be okay with him.

Only he'd done a damn shitty job so far.

The next step would be to figure out what project to do and let her do it. So now what would transform her from being an unwilling participant to a willing one?

A slow smile crossed his face as he picked up the paper he'd been using for doodles and folded it once then twice. His smile widened. He finally understood one thing – the theme of the project. This was all about transformation.

CHAPTER 6

Tuesday

THE NEXT MORNING, Paris took her seat beside Weaver, giving him the briefest of glances. He was waiting for her. Before she could say anything, he said in an apologetic tone, "I'm sorry. I didn't mean to upset you."

Then he placed a small folded bird on her desk. She was charmed at the delicate wings and precise features of the tiny bird. In order to create something so beautiful and fragile, there had to be something soft under that hard exterior of his. The gift wasn't enough to forgive him, but it helped to break the awkwardness of their first meeting since the fight.

"It's okay. I'm still not happy about it, but I understand."

"You do?" he asked, startled.

Nodding, she explained. "I do. I don't want to be in any report, but I understand that you need to write one."

He kept his head down as if in deep thought, as if her answer was what he wanted to hear but maybe just not quite the right way. Well, too damn bad. She understood his machinations more than he did apparently. He'd been studying other people so much, Weaver had forgotten to look closer to home.

Paris, on the other hand, had started with herself and had gone on from there. Already she had learned a lot, but there was more. She felt it. Who knew what she'd learn as she moved into studying other people? She'd come willing to learn but damn, this project business had shaken her.

And that upset her too.

Still, the desperation to get what healing she could kept her here. Even if that meant working with someone who wasn't ready to heal.

"What about our project?" she muttered. "I'd feel better if I knew what direction we were supposed to take."

"I was thinking about a report on transformation."

As he spoke, he pointed to the origami bird. "We both need to learn to grow. To change. Theoretically, to transform. From the old to the new. Whether by understanding how our stance on any issue, justice included, can be muted to something else or by looking past another person's point of view or something else entirely unrelated."

"True," she said slowly. "But that is a word. Transformation. What would we do the report about?"

"About how we have transformed ourselves so far and where we want to go. Maybe put it into stages. One, being where we've been. Two, being where we are. And three, being where we have to go."

Warming to his concept, she listened as he fleshed it out further. "Use Justice as the vehicle."

"Sounds good, but honestly that's just self-analysis. Hardly the scope of what Jenna wants out of us." Paris knew that a project like this could be difficult, but she'd expected something different. Something more public. In public. Dealing with people. At least Sean and Robin's had been. She'd heard about Kane and Tania's project from Robin, but not the details. They'd only had to go into the public for Tania to take pictures. So maybe that was internal too. She didn't know.

"Maybe that would be okay." She shrugged. "Let's ask Jenna about it."

"Why?"

"Because I don't want to do anything wrong or waste time going off in one direction that we're just going to have to redo it."

"And I don't want to ask because if we do, we're opening ourselves up to it being wrong," he countered. "Whereas if we leave it and do the project the best we can, it won't be wrong. It will be our interpretation of the project."

"You don't like being wrong," she said with a wry smile. "So you ignore the process and decide you're right from your perspective."

"And you're scared of being wrong so you go and ask over every little stage to make sure you aren't."

That was dead on. She sat back, surprised. "Wow, this could be tough working with you."

"And you," he came back with immediately.

Both leaned back, smiles breaking to the surface.

At least it gave them a place to start. If needed, she could go ask Jenna on her own, and if they could improve on this project, then she'd have to convince Weaver to make those changes and if not, she'd have to make a decision. He was right in that she didn't like making mistakes. She'd grown up crippled, her doubts exaggerated by severe punishments when she'd done something wrong. Now she asked a lot of questions early on so she understood what was required of her. Whereas, Weaver refused to be wrong – as if that mental leap was too much for him to handle.

Maybe the same end result. Just different methodologies. As long as they both managed to avoid triggering the memories of what happened to them when they were wrong, then it all worked.

But it also said that he had a lot more stuff going on in his history than he was willing to look at. Could she help him? Should she help him? Would he let her help him?

And how did that do anything for her? She was greedy. She wanted the progress for herself. Not necessarily for him unless she also progressed. She didn't want to slow anyone down, but neither did she want to be left behind. Her eagerness for this course had been all-encompassing and now here she was feeling flat and let down.

Once again it was like she'd asked for too much, hoped for too much, and reality, the bitch, had already let her down. Then again, what did she expect? There weren't any miracles in her life, remember? Miracles were only for people who deserved them.

Sean had found his miracle. Her brother Sean found Robin. Not that he'd say they were a hit right off. He'd seen how damaged Robin had been at the time and had moved forward *with* her.

Now it was Paris's turn, and she wanted a similar result. If not a partner, at least major growth. Could Jenna pull off magic a third time?

Dispirited, she looked around at the seminar room turned classroom and realized she didn't want to be here. She'd come with such high expectations, foolish ones, and foolish of her, but she'd been so wanting to be here and now that there was no sign of stardust in the air, she wanted to go home. Another one of her patterns. If she didn't like something, didn't look like it was going to lead her in the right direction, then she wanted to quit.

Why waste her time? She didn't have the laid back personality of her brother. She was driven to succeed. Driven to go after what she wanted in life. Whatever that was. Right now it was healing.

Was she just being impatient? After all, the workshop had just started, but it didn't feel like impatience. It felt like she'd taken a wrong turn somewhere, but she didn't know where.

Why wasn't it coming together for her?

PARIS WAS WIRED. Not the way he was wired internally, but wired as in needy and determined to get those needs filled. Because of that, sitting slumped with her eyes closed, he figured she was getting depressed.

Interesting mix again. The lack of direction in the report bugged her. He could understand that. No one wanted to waste time, but he doubted they were as anal about it as she appeared to be. Still, she was right. They didn't have time to redo the report if they were off on the wrong tangent.

How to make this work. He stared down at the notes he'd been so happy with earlier that now looked like shit. He hated that. "Okay, let's ask Jenna for more help."

Her gaze widened and she spun around to stare at him. "Really? Okay, let's catch her as she comes in."

"Uh…" But she was gone.

Holy crap. Not wanting to be excluded from anything, he forced himself up, smiled apologetically at the others, and walked over to where Paris waited. "This is hardly the time," he muttered.

"There is no time. The seminar is already in progress. We've been here one night already. We need to get on the ball."

The eagerness in her voice surprised him. Driven was one thing, but this was a workshop. Sit back and relax, do a few assignments and carry on.

Not for her. And if he was going to get in her way, she'd run him over. "Why are you in such a hurry?"

She frowned at him. "You just don't get it, do you? We're all here for a reason. Each of us. Unlike you."

"Hey," he protested, "I'm here for a reason."

"Not one that is about healing or moving forward in your life." She snorted. "You're trying to climb the academic ladder rather than work on your life. That would be too hard. Much easier to hold your report up as an excuse instead of admitting that you have as much to work on as the rest of us."

Just then, she caught sight of Jenna and ran toward her, leaving Weaver in shock staring behind her. "How did she know that," he muttered to the empty hallway.

Only it wasn't empty. One of the women working at the hotel smiled at him as she walked past, her arms full of paper. "One of the things we've always seen here on Jenna's workshops," she said, "is transformation. People come here from one mindset and go home with another."

As her heels clicked down the sparkling hallway, he stared after her, his thoughts full of his earlier contemplations on the report. Transformation again.

The more he thought about it, he realized it didn't fit Paris. Because she wasn't waiting for transformation to happen, she was going to *make* it happen, and that didn't work in his mind. Transformation to him was something that happened inside. When you weren't looking. As if it were something that went on at very deep levels of consciousness and then when you turned around one day, you were at a completely different state of awareness.

Paris wasn't about that. There was an edge of desperation to her actions. As if she was afraid that it wasn't going to happen. That whatever good could come out of this workshop would pass her by. That was not something she could live with. For her, it was time for change, any way she could get it.

As the last phrase slipped through his mental preamble, he realized that was the one that fit. There was an edge of righteousness to her actions. She deserved this. She'd worked for it. Been through a lot to get it, and now was afraid it wasn't there for her.

Or maybe she wanted to deserve it, but inside maybe she didn't really believe it. That's why the desperation.

He wondered if Jenna knew. That was one cagey woman. The insights she had into people's character was something he'd never seen and Weaver wondered, given his own blocks, if he ever would.

Paris made him feel a little ashamed. He didn't give a damn about moving forward. The place he was at right now was safe and he wanted to stay there.

Wow. Wincing, he figured that maybe they were a great pair after all.

He didn't want to move forward, and she couldn't stay where she was.

And they still had no plan of action.

Maybe that all related back to the transformation lesson again. Maybe they'd turn around and it would have happened at that inner level while they weren't looking. He'd love that. To move from where he sat to another major step without really knowing what he'd done, but in truth, life wasn't like that. These steps were painful. Huge and difficult. That's why he wasn't interested in going to another one – at least not right now.

Paris was too desperate. He understood that something drove that desperation, but it made it hard to watch her. Great. Of course he had a whole week of being with her. Like it or not, Jenna had a reason for everything she did. And he doubted this pairing was any different.

And why the hell did Paris have to be so interesting?

A relationship with someone in therapy was a bad idea. Look where the last one had left him.

Alone and divorced.

There was no way he was going through that again.

CHAPTER 7

PARIS BOLTED DOWN the hallway toward Jenna. It seemed since she'd arrived this week she hadn't been able to walk anywhere. Something was always sending her forward at top speed, trying to get to where she was going and getting precisely nowhere. It was making her desperate and crazy.

"Jenna, we need help with this project."

Jenna stopped in the hallway, her gaze amused but calm. "Do you?"

"Yes." Paris nodded vigorously. "We do."

"We?"

Paris glanced behind her. Damn Weaver, where are you? "Sorry, I thought Weaver was coming to see you, too."

"Hmmm." Jenna studied Paris. "What part do you need help with?"

"The beginning." Paris hated the crippling feeling inside. That need to get it right. "I can't start," she said, then corrected her statement. "I don't know where to start."

"Did you come up with a theme?"

"Too many of them. Black and White. Right or Wrong. Justice. Transformation. That seems to be a major trigger point for both of us."

"Right and wrong, black and white, and Justice could be pretty much the same theme, so all of them could work."

Paris could feel the hot words bubbling up. "I don't want something that *could* work. I want the *right* one. I need this to work," she cried. And then she gasped, falling silent, shocked at her own words.

After a long moment, she muttered, "I'm sorry."

"Don't be," Jenna said in a sober tone. "I think that was something that needed to come out for a long time." Jenna shifted the books in her arms and studied her closer. "This is an important issue. Remember, desperation often pushes away what you need most." She looked doubtful for a long moment, and Paris remembered the conversation where she'd damn near begged to be let into the seminar. Desperate then, too.

"I'm sorry. I'm sorry," she said, "I don't mean to be."

"No, but it's that very need inside you that needs to be addressed. You can't heal if you can't let go. So what do you need to let go of so you aren't so desperate to move forward?"

"Fear." The word popped out instantly. "Fear of not getting the same benefit out of the seminar that my brother did. Fear of ..." she took a deep breath and let it fly. "Failing. Of once again not being good enough. Not good enough to be loved. To love. Being so horrible, so bad, so much a failure that no one will ever love me."

Her voice broke around her, the words splintering like icicles. Each hitting her skin like tiny pinpricks and making her bleed, and still the pain boiled over. "I tried so hard to be good. And I was never able to be good *enough*. He still beat on me every chance he got."

Tears flooded her eyes as the memories flooded her mind. This was not the place to break down. Not here. Not like this. Panicked to get away, she turned and ran.

Up the two flights of stairs, then down the hallway. The carpet in front of her was a blur. Instinct led her home. She made it to her room and got it unlocked, but it was a struggle. Moving at all was difficult. Inside her head, all she could hear were the words – *another failure.*

"Easy, Paris. You're fine. You're here at the hotel. No one else can see you."

Paris stiffened. It was Weaver.

Then she felt strong arms around her. She cringed, an instinctive reaction, still caught in the gray shadows of the memories.

His hands dropped away.

With tears in her eyes she waited, a sense of fatalism in her heart, knowing the blows that would come. He'd hit her next. Knock her to the ground and kick her until she couldn't get up again. She shuddered, feeling the film of sweat coating her skin. The waves of greasy pain ready to rise from her gut. And still nothing. Then she heard him beside her.

She shuddered again.

"I'm not going to hurt you," he whispered. "Never would I hit you."

The words rolled over her in a wave of disbelief as she shifted through time from her childhood to the seminar and the hallway where she stood like an idiot. Eyes shut tight, her body swaying in reaction, feeling flushed with realization. Oh Lord. It was Weaver next to her, not her father. Paralyzed, only a sob escaped.

Once again he wrapped his arm around her, turned her around, and tugged her up against his chest. She went stiff with fear. But this time he didn't let go. Her heart thumped. She knew better than to fight. But he just held her. Gently.

The gentleness was her undoing. The tears that burned her eyes burst forth and tumbled free, the waterfall gaining momentum as it poured down her cheeks and soaked his shirt.

Emotions washed through her, the onslaught so hard and fast, she couldn't move.

The primary emotion that beat as loudly as her heart was disbelief.

It had been a long time since she had had an episode like that. She'd hoped to never be crippled by those memories again. Somehow she'd failed. Somehow they'd snuck in from behind, waiting for her to fall to pieces.

And of course she had. With Jenna – her very words releasing the flood she'd worked so hard to keep dammed up.

Caught in the maelstrom, she didn't notice the soothing touch up and down her back for a long time. It was Weaver. Being nice. The only other person to treat her like this was Sean. Her beloved brother. Without him, she wouldn't have survived her childhood. She knew he felt that she'd returned the favor but she hadn't – not really.

"Feeling better?" Weaver's voice was deep…clogged.

Not wanting to show him her puffy face, she frowned and looked down. But he wouldn't let her hide. He tucked a finger under her chin and slowly lifted her face toward him.

She tried to pull free. He let her.

"You shouldn't hide your emotions, you know. They are honest and therefore beautiful," he said in such a pensive voice she couldn't take umbrage with him, but his words did startle a laugh out of her.

"Maybe honest, but also downright ugly." She pulled out of his arms and dashed into the bedroom then the bathroom to the side. There she stared into the big mirror. Red splotchy skin and eyes too big for her face. It went along with the equally large mouth. But her eyes glowed. Tear-rinsed and shiny, she wondered if the release of emotion might have made them look better.

"Maybe I should cry more often," she muttered. "Not." She took a moment to use the facilities then used cold water to rinse her face, hoping to ease back the puffiness. When she figured she'd waited long enough for him to have left, she opened the door and walked out.

He stepped up beside her.

Shit.

"NO, DON'T AVOID me, please."

She turned her face away.

He sighed. "You look fine now."

Laughter bubbled out from Paris's mouth. Weaver was delighted to realize it was real. He grinned. "Okay, let me amend that. You look great for having just been through a crying jag."

"That's better, I suppose," she muttered. "My face always looks so horrible when I've been crying."

"Well, it's over and time to fix the rest." At her honest smile, he added. "I don't suppose you'd like to tell me what brought tha—"

Before he could finish she was shaking her head, stopping his question. "No."

He lifted his shoulders in surrender. "I was just hoping to not trigger it again."

"You didn't," she said. "Jenna did."

"Oh." Well, that's what she was supposed to do, and

likely it was a private matter that he was never going to know about. Damn it. Although he'd planned to stay detached and separated from everyone attending, he was finding that wasn't likely going to happen any time soon – not from Paris.

She wiped her eyes and said in a muffled voice, "I think I'll stay in my room."

"Or we can go back to the seminar and get through the afternoon session like the trooper you are."

Her smile was still watery but it was normal. "I look like a mess."

"And you won't be alone. That's why we all came, re-member?" He studied her, watching her gaze narrow and turn direct.

"Is that why you came?" she challenged. "I thought it was for your stupid publication."

"You forget, I'm damaged too. Whether this was my choice or not or whether the seminar works isn't the issue. One can't be here in a setting like this, with healing going on, without having change happen within your own psyche. Maybe I didn't come prepared with a big issue I was hoping to overcome, but I'm going to come up against issues regardless. Life is like that."

He might have forgotten that point too along the way but being here now like he was, watching her, dealing with the repercussions of his report, being around growth, well, he wouldn't be able to escape. He remembered that now. It really didn't matter. He'd move forward one painful step at a time – whether he liked it or not.

CHAPTER 8

THE AFTERNOON SEMINAR moved quickly, being mostly group activities. They were easier to do and allowed Paris to pull back inside her shield so the world wasn't scraping her raw. There was a lot she could do to protect herself.

By the time they were almost done, Jenna called out, "For the next hour, work in pairs on your project."

She stood up. "Paris and Weaver, come up here please and we'll discuss yours."

"Oh finally." Paris bounded to her feet without looking to see if Weaver was coming or not. She stood in front of Jenna's desk. "Thanks."

Jenna smiled. "Take a seat, both of you."

That's when Paris noticed Weaver standing behind her. "Oh, sorry." She scooted to the side and sat down. Weaver sat in the other chair.

"Did you come up with a theme yet, you two?"

Paris shook her head. Weaver nodded.

Jenna smiled. "So one says yes and one says no. Interesting. Okay. Paris, have you heard what Weaver has come up with?"

Paris frowned at Weaver. "I don't think so."

Weaver shrugged. "No big deal. I was going to suggest transformation."

"Oh, I did hear that," Paris admitted.

There was silence as both women contemplated the theme.

"But what would we do with it?" Paris asked. "I'm not against that, I just don't understand how to use it for a report. Short of explaining how I've seen my life transformed."

She slid a sideways glance over at Jenna, who was moving a pen between her fingers, deep in thought.

That would be an easier project to do than some and would trigger a lot of memories. Some not so easy to deal with. That can of worms was better left unopened.

"Maybe we should define that more," Jenna said. "Not your life per se, but how one incident, a huge incident in your life, has affected every day you've lived since." Her gaze was direct, warm, caring and....shit....*determined* as she looked at Paris.

"In fact, I think it needs to be that really big white elephant each of us has in our lives that we don't want to talk about. That we don't want anyone in this room to know about." She waited a beat then added, "But that needs to come out."

"If we've acknowledged this incident as a problem, then sharing it with others is both unnecessary and painful," Weaver said.

"And can't happen," Paris blurted out. Jenna knew she couldn't deal with this. It wasn't possible for Paris to talk about it. She couldn't. The familiar tightening on her chest, her inability to breathe, these were more than feelings. They were real. Her eyes closed and she focused on the next breath. Just one. If she could get that one out – there – she did it. Then the next one, then the next one. By the time she opened her eyes, she realized that there was only silence around her as the others watched.

"It really sends you into a panic attack, doesn't it," Weaver asked.

She nodded.

"That's the big one then. You so have to let that go. The fear will kill you," he said seriously.

She gazed off into the distance. "But I know what it is, I know what happened, putting that into a project isn't going to help me – it will traumatize me. And I wasn't alone. I don't feel that I can share what happened without breaking a confidence in someone else. They need their privacy too."

"Use a different name?" Weaver suggested.

"No, he'd still be obvious. You'd know who he was." She thought about it. "And it's too big."

"Big is good," Weaver said. "It gives you lots to work with."

"No, like this is huge. I can't deal with this. It's too hard." Paris pleaded.

Silence.

Jenna spoke up, her voice warm and fuzzy, "Then deal with a layer on top. That will make the big issue a little easier for you to access, and yet you'll feel better for having gotten something done. Some level of pain gone."

"A top layer?"

"Yes." Jenna waited a moment. "How about the fear of not being good enough. Not deserving enough to get what you want in life."

That did it. Frozen again, her breath locked down. Jenna was referring to Paris's outburst this morning, when she'd almost lost it completely, and didn't it damn well figure that Jenna would pick up on that one horrible, crippling aspect.

She struggled to take a breath, that oh-so-very necessary air into her lungs so she could take another breath – one that would allow her to fight the good fight and keep living for another day.

Heat radiated up her arm as she became aware of fingers gently stroking her skin, soothing her panic, easing back the rough edges of her control.

A gasping, raspy breath escaped.

"Sure," she heard herself mention sarcastically. "Like that isn't a big one."

"Good." Jenna stood up, deliberately misunderstanding her, and said, "That's settled. Find a way to visually express your transformation." And she collected her books and walked out, leaving Paris staring after her.

"Visually?" Weaver said. "Really?"

"That's what she said. Although how does one visually represent the fear of not being good enough? Not deserving enough have to do with anything?"

"I think she left us some latitude in there, but still."

Feeling more balanced, Paris shot a look around the room, but no one noticed. They were all packing up to leave. She planned to do that too. Just as soon as she could get her body to move.

WEAVER HAD SEEN several people have panic attacks but hadn't realized that Paris was crippled so severely by them. Jenna had certainly hit it on the head about what Paris's big dominating issue was. At least the one that was accessible. And she was right, one had to deal with the little bits and reduce the pain and fear around the big one until it was manageable.

Then when it least surprised you, that one opened up because you came from a position of strength now and it had been weakened. He could hope for such a breakthrough for her. She deserved it.

"What about at your work?" he asked curiously. "Is there anything there that would show you something visual in transforming? You deal with mothers and babies, correct?"

She nodded, a gentle smile on her face. "I do love my work. Helping the women yes, but seeing the babies, working with the ones that have a tough time and seeing them survive and thrive…" Her smile grew misty. "It's special."

"And the ones that don't survive?" he asked. How could she deal with the loss of babies like that? That would be too much for him, he was too big a softie.

"I cry," she said simply. "A lot. But never there. Never at work. I make it through my day – sad but functioning – then I go home and I cry for them. There's nothing else I can do. In many cases I have to wonder if it wasn't a blessing as the poor little things were in such pain and it wasn't going to get much better, but then I remember some that have struggled so hard and have done well…" she smiled, "and I remember that all we can do is fight. Sometimes we win and sometimes we lose."

"That's not a bad way to look at life in general." Weaver smiled. "Even now, today. We have a project to do. Let's apply that common sense to making it happen."

"I don't have a problem doing the work," Paris replied, "but once again I don't know where to start."

"That's always the hardest place," he said, "but the good thing is, in this case, you've already started!"

It took a moment for a small frown on her forehead to

clear, and then she smiled. "That's true, but not very helpful."

He laughed. "Hey, whatever works. Sometimes I do the end of the report because I know that's where I'm going. I then backtrack to the beginning to lay down the steps required to get there."

"That's actually not a bad idea." Her face brightened. "I'll have to think about that."

"Good. In the meantime, how about a walk?" He could see the refusal forming on her face, he jumped in to add, "Nothing long, just out in the gardens or around the dock." He snagged her elbow. "Let's go."

CHAPTER 9

PARIS HAD NO desire to go out, to leave her safety net. Weaver wasn't giving her a choice. Before she understood what had happened, she was standing outside the hotel in downtown Vancouver, her jacket on, and staring up at the windy gray skies. It matched her mood. The emotions rocking her today were enough to make her tired, depressed. She hated the toll it was taking on her. It's like someone took all the stuffing out of her and just when she thought the bad stuff was all gone, she realized it was only a drop in the ocean of bad still waiting for her to deal with.

"I wonder if everyone has something major to deal with?"

"Everyone has *something* to deal with. The term 'major' is subjective. Trying to buy a new car and not sure how to could be construed as a major problem in some people's eyes."

She snorted. "I wish."

"Come on, let's walk."

It was the last thing she wanted to do, but her feet had a mind of their own and fell into step beside him. The air was cool for a September day. The moist, slightly salty air revitalized her spirits. Normally the spring and fall here were warm and stunningly beautiful with bright blue skies. Today offered the beautiful part, but it wasn't warm or blue. She stuffed her hands into her jacket pockets and let the world stroll by as she walked.

"We'll head towards the ocean."

"Wherever." She shrugged.

"Are you cold?" he asked in concern. "The breeze has a bite to it."

"I'm fine," she murmured. "It's cool but refreshing."

They walked in silence until the first glimpses of the sailboats popped into view. She broke into laughter. "They always look so bright and cheerful out there buffeted by the wind and waves."

"I don't know how cheerful they are today considering the beating they are taking."

The breeze that brushed by them was a strong wind out in the bay, but the people in the sailboats looked to be having the time of their lives. Then she caught sight of the kite surfers. "What a sport," she exclaimed.

"Looks like fun, but so not for me."

"Not into dangerous sports?" she asked, feeling shivers sliding over her skin. "I'm not either, but men generally like that sort of thing." Of course her brother didn't, but in their house, growing up had been a dangerous sport. She smiled, loving the reminder of her brother, and the shivers stopped.

"Not my style." He gave a harsh laugh and said, "I survived childhood. That was hard enough."

Shocked, she stopped all of a sudden, then turned to look at him. "I was just thinking the same thing."

With an understanding look, he moved closer to her. "Our daily life isn't like these people." He pointed out a particularly high-flying kite boarder. "He's happy to chase after excitement and danger. For most of us who grew up in a violent household, we are looking for the opposite. We want peace and safety now."

She couldn't have said it better. The insight into his life, his childhood, made her realize he really had been through the wringer – like the rest of them at the seminar. Holding her breath, she stayed silent, hoping he'd share more. One foot rested on the cement barricade between them and the water, the look on his face distant but calm. As if he'd come to terms with something behind him.

She wished.

There was a world of difference between his childhood and hers, she knew, but for the first time she realized there was also a lot in common.

"Maybe some of those people have been hurt so much they no longer care what happens to them?"

"That's the other side of the coin, isn't it?" He glanced at her. "Survival means different things to different people. Some say they survived, but inside they are dead and can't stand living. Some people do crazy stunts in the hope to kill themselves off because they aren't strong enough to do it themselves. Sounds horrible, but I've seen it."

"And in some cases, they are so angry inside they turn around and inflict the same abuse on others," Paris whispered, looking at the black mark his shoe scuffed into the cement barricade. Briefly letting her gaze follow the line of his foot up his leg, remembering how it felt when he had held her.

She didn't see the same rage in his demeanor or actions she'd seen in other men. He'd never hit anyone for fun. Was she right to trust that assumption? She didn't really know him. But she wanted to.

"Often those people feel that they have to get their own back. Or feel like if it happened to them, why should you be safe? I knew one male who figured it was his job to go around and attack women because then they wouldn't be so trusting. They'd take more precautions because now they understood life could be dangerous."

"Really? That's a little twisted, isn't it?" Startled, his words shook her out of her daze. She'd read about a lot of people and their odd reactions to stress and pain, but that was a new one on her.

"There are some very sad cases out there."

"And here," she muttered.

"As long as we do what we can."

"Everyone is doing what they can," she said quietly. "Even those still locked in that same horrible place they went to during the abuse. And they can't move out of there because it's either too painful or fear won't let them move. Either way, it's all they can do, too." Quiet, Paris wondered at what she'd started. What she'd inadvertently shared.

"You've been there?" Weaver questioned.

"All my childhood and teen years. I should have run away. Should have gotten help. I couldn't." Hands jammed in her pockets, she tried to still the shakes rattling her calm.

"It's easy to look back. Not so easy to avoid judging."

"Sometimes I think looking back is all about judging. What we could have done differently. What we should have done differently."

"Except…" Glancing down at her, their eyes met, "we have to make allowances for the age we were back then. The conditioning we were put through."

"And when we were older and still allowed the status quo to remain? Then what?" The bitterness in her voice was audible. She bit her lip "I stopped it – finally. I should have done it earlier."

"And how old were you when you stopped it?"

It took a long time for her to answer, and then with a sigh, she said, "Fifteen."

His shocked gasp made her look at him sharply, searching for the judgment she expected to see. And there was none. Still she felt she had to explain more, to justify herself. Her actions. "No, I wasn't very old, but I was old enough. And if I'd done something about it earlier, then someone else wouldn't have gotten so very badly hurt."

"You were a child. Before and during. The conditioning you were put through didn't give you the tools to handle resistance, to defend yourself or to stand up for someone else. We're usually so broken by the time we get there it takes a major turning point in our lives to make us change. In your case, maybe for this other person."

She gave him a hooded look. "More book learning?"

"No, life learning." And this time, it was him that turned away.

Something to think about. She sagged onto the railing and studied his averted face. "Life's a bitch, isn't it?"

That surprised a laugh out of him. "Isn't it though? Or maybe I should say, life used to be a bitch. Now it's much better."

"True." A young couple walked past them, holding hands and lost inside the joy of their young love. Jealousy rose up at the sight of them, and yet at the same time she wasn't sure she'd ever want to be so naive. She'd never been that innocent. Not like they were. And once you crossed a certain point, there was no going back. "Do you ever look at the people around us and wonder what we missed?" she asked.

"Yes." He studied the same couple as they passed by,

murmuring with their heads close to together. "I'd like to look at it as what we still have waiting for us to experience."

"So not a missed opportunity, but rather in the future as something to look forward to?" The concept of not having missed anything wasn't something Paris had considered. But it was a much nicer way to look at the issue. "I can get on board with that."

The implication of what he'd said dawned on her. Her lips parted to ask him, then she realized how deeply personal a question it was. She closed her mouth.

"Go ahead and ask," he said simply. "I may or may not answer."

"That's fair enough. It's just what you said, the way you said it, while that couple walked by…"

"And…" His voice tightened just enough to let her know he sensed where she was going.

"Nothing." Losing the courage to go there, she shrugged and stood up. "Shall we keep walking?"

"Sure." They headed down the walkway in the opposite direction the couple had gone. Kinda like the way their lives had gone in the opposite direction.

"You were going to ask about the relationships in my life."

Startled, she glanced at him quickly then seeing his intent gaze, she switched to watching one sailboat trying to come back to shore, and a shiver crawled up her spine. Struggling but winning the war. Prophetic in many ways. "I guess I was. Just trying to figure out how trust works after there is none."

"It doesn't. That's why you have to start from scratch and build new trust in different things. When you've been hurt, then you try to avoid being hurt again. When you've been broken, you avoid anything that will take you down that path a second time."

Once again his words hit home. "So true. But that doesn't allow much room for trust."

"So you have to trust that people will be people. What you're really asking me is have I come to the point of trusting other people to not hurt me."

She winced. "It always comes back to being hurt."

"Sure. That's the big lesson in life – to go on even though we've been hurt. So trust in little bits. Trust your coworkers to treat you nicely. Trust your boss to be fair. Trust babies to be natural. Natural at that age is to be innocent, but they learn manipulation at a young age."

"They do at that." Paris smiled, thinking about the babies at work. "I love that about children. But when they hurt someone, they also feel bad."

"In most cases."

"But from there to becoming adults, people change. And that can be a different story."

"That is their issue. Remember, it's always about you and your issues."

"I want a family," she burst out. "Children."

Then went silent.

THE VEHEMENCE IN her voice startled him. "Surely that's not a bad thing?"

She bowed her head.

"I think that would be a dream many women would have," he offered gently, wondering where this was going.

"Sure they do." With a shrug of her shoulders, her tone bitter, she added, "But I'm not most women."

That's for sure, but he understood. "Maybe adopt if you don't feel the conventional way would work for you?"

"I'm considering it," she said slowly. "I've seen many single moms come through my ward. Most aren't in good shape either emotionally or financially. A few are strong and planned this journey to walk alone, but most aren't as they've come from recent breakups or relationships where they couldn't even remember the father."

"Not everything in life is so sad," he said.

"No," she whispered. "The babies are awesome. They are born so innocent and open to what life has to offer."

"Do you deal with a lower income level demographic that you see so many upsetting scenarios?"

"Not especially, and money doesn't protect you from breakups." Staring down at her hands, she sighed. "There is no guarantee that your relationship or your spouse will survive your children making it to adulthood. Few people go into a relationship expecting to become a single parent. Often they come with the disintegration of their own dreams, a major shift in their reality. Their circumstances." She raised her gaze. "And sometimes I envy them, regardless."

"Can't you have children?" Immediately he winced, wishing he held his tongue when her face paled to the whitest cloud in the sky and those huge eyes swelled with tears.

As she shook her head, he hated himself for not having read the signs. Hell, in her case, he hadn't been able to read any signs. Something about her blurred his usual logic and calm deference. He'd been lost on that highway like an idiot. "I'm so sorry."

Purposefully taking a breath, she nodded, sniffled, and

then shrugged. "It's not news for me, I've known for a long time."

Moodily, he stared out over the water, recognizing that the storm clouds now looked to be ready to dump its load of rain on Vancouver. "So often it's that way, isn't it? When we really want something, we see others not giving value to what we want so badly."

"That's when my job is difficult. Although it's also joyful and rewarding, it's painful," she admitted. "I've thought of changing jobs so I'm not around the babies all the time, but it's hard. I do love them and as I'm never going to be able to have one, at least this way I can be close to them."

"What about a surrogate? Although I guess that's not a guaranteed path of success either. Adoption is likely the best route. From another country maybe?"

Again he spoke off the top of his head, without his usual internal edit. He glanced at her, wondering if adoption was even an option. For many women, it wouldn't be.

"I've been looking into it," she said, "but that whole single motherhood thing is a problem again. Not an impossibility, but definitely a challenge."

"Is that why you're here?"

She turned to stare at him, her gaze flat, shuttered. "That's partly why I'm here. Anything that allows me to gain acceptance of this aspect of my life is always a benefit, but no, that's not the biggest thing." This time she winced and went quiet.

Really quiet.

Watching her, as her gaze remained fixated at her feet, he had no idea how to broach the silence. So far she'd been very open with him, and if he could just keep her talking, they'd have an easier time of it this week. But she wasn't giving him much in the way of openings.

Then again, neither had he told her about his life either.

"I was married once." Shit. Where had that come from? He hadn't planned on that, but the words just slipped out.

"Good for you," she said in a noncommittal voice, as if it didn't mean anything. And he guessed in the current world of relationships where a person was often married two or three times in their lifetime, maybe it didn't.

But for him, it had been major.

"It lasted six months."

She gasped and turned towards him. "What? Why?"

Angry with himself mentioning it, he shrugged and tried to look nonchalant. He'd done it now.

"I thought I could handle it. She thought she could handle it."

"And…?"

It was his turn to look down at his feet and he paused before replying. "We were both wrong."

And then she had to do it. She asked, "Handle what?"

CHAPTER 10

IT WAS MAJOR that he'd even brought up something so personal, and now she was dying with curiosity. That she'd spoken so openly said much about this conversation. Normally she'd never have said a word, but he was part of the week and somehow that made a difference. Besides, he obviously had problems himself.

Maybe he'd share them or maybe not, but he'd come a long ways already this morning. But oh Lord. Married for only six months?

"How long had you known each other?" Shit, she shouldn't have asked. It was none of her business. Seriously none of her business. Yet he'd brought it up and she was relieved to not be the one under scrutiny for a change.

"Months. But she was in therapy and hadn't progressed as far as I thought she had."

For some reason, that tone of his made her back go up. "And you?" she asked. "Had you progressed as far as you thought?"

His shoulders slumped, and for a long time she thought he wouldn't answer. "Obviously not. I couldn't persuade her to stay with me."

"Ouch," she murmured. "Well, at least you made it to the altar." Walking back to the hotel, her words surprised her and her cheeks flushed. "I never made it to bed."

She felt his startled response. Heard his strangled exclamation and ignored his question, "Really?"

He raced to keep up to her. "Why not?"

"For the same reason I can't have kids and the same reason I can't get past all the other lovely issues in my life."

There was a strong silence that almost made her smile. Hell, her honesty was making her smile. Normally she would never have let it all out. Maybe because she was at the workshop – and she wouldn't see Weaver again. That was what this whole week was all about, wasn't it?

She frowned. "How come I haven't seen you around Jenna's evening classes? Normally these workshops are full of her students."

"I haven't been to her evening sessions lately."

"Did she help you?"

There was pause before he answered, "Yes in that every person on our path helps each of us. She triggered a lot of issues. I met her after my wife and I broke up. So I needed the new perspective. The awareness that came from a few things she said."

"Yeah, she's good at that."

"I know this is intensely personal but I have to ask, do you mean to say you have never had a sexual relationship?"

This time she looked right at him. "The way you mean, no." She picked up the pace. The hotel should be around the corner. Not close enough, but it was her fault for bringing up the personal questions in the first place.

Glancing over at him, she could see him desperately wanting to ask more but not knowing how. "What you really want to know is what happened so I avoid men?" At his nod, she said, "I won't be sharing that until you're ready to share your mess. However, I was never raped, if that's what you're thinking, but there are things that can happen to you that are much worse."

Half shocked at what she said but mostly shocked at her ability to go there and still breathe, she turned, ready to bolt toward the hotel. When he grabbed her arm, she froze.

"Look, I'm sorry. Curiosity is natural, but it can also be destructive. I do understand that before growth comes the breaking down of barriers." Weaver said with a sigh and looked toward the hotel. "I only want you to tell me what you want to tell. I'm a good listener."

"But not necessarily someone who plans to grow past your own issues." With a tight smile, she pulled away from his grasp. "It's one thing to share and have sharing go both ways. It's another thing to talk to a therapist." She turned her back on him. "I have Jenna for the latter position already. Thanks though," she said with excruciating care. "I'll find someone else to do the sharing thing with."

Looking forward, she picked up her footsteps and ran.

Part of her never wanted to see him again. Yet part of her wanted him to follow. But why would he? He'd have to step up and be himself. A workshop participant was all about giving and taking. And she doubted he was up for much more of it.

Putting him firmly out of her mind, she rushed inside the front entrance, blind to the group milling about. There were so many she had to slip around people to get where she needed to go. She was getting hungry, but the restaurant was looking overwhelmingly full. Damn.

Why now?

Finally, she managed to reach the wall of elevators and came up against a huge billboard standing between the elevators. The boards were full of information, but her gaze was caught on the one word at the top. Justice.

Jesus. Like she needed more of that.

Her heart pounded and tears filled her eyes. She turned in slow motion to realize many of the people there were in uniform. Police uniforms. Some men wore suits, but all carried themselves the same way. The place was filled with cops. There was no room to stand, let alone breathe.

Then she caught sight of one man's profile. Her heart stalled then raced ahead as if trying to reach safety before the rest of her could. Please don't let it be him. Not now. Not here.

His features came up sharper. Dear God.

She closed her eyes and very slowly turned to face the elevators. Her feet were screaming at her to run. Now.

She bolted for the stairs.

Just as she disappeared around the corner, she heard someone call her name.

Blind, her only objective to get inside her room, alone, she ran. Faster.

WEAVER WATCHED PARIS disappear from sight.

Now what the hell was going on? Paris was continuing her confusing mix of personalities. Just when she began to open up and share, only when it got seriously interesting, she shut off the valve. And he really wanted to know the rest of it. It was not in him to leave a woman walking alone in Vancouver on the streets, and he'd kept up with her flight. Back at the hotel, he'd seen her make her way through the crowd. Being tall, he'd easily tracked her progress to the elevators. But he couldn't see the reason for her sudden bolt up the stairs. Was she claustrophobic? He hadn't seen signs of it before, but then again, the crowd here was intense.

Some kind of law enforcement seminar was going on. Cool.

He managed to find his way through the crowd to the stairs and followed her up.

There were others going ahead of him. He hated being worried about her, but there was something about that eager beaver attitude and wanting-to-make-her-life-happen innocence that was begging for trouble. She'd seen a lot in her life already, but damn he didn't want her to be hit with more.

Weaver followed her up to the fourth floor, but by the time he got up there, the hall was empty. She must have made it to the safety of her room already.

Inside his room, he tossed his light jacket over the back of his chair when someone knocked on his door. He went to answer it, only to find it hadn't been on his door but on the room across the hall. The older man in a police uniform turned to look. Weaver smiled and went to close the door.

The man called out, "Paris, are you in there? I know you likely don't remember me..."

Silence.

"I was hoping to meet you now that I know you are here."

More silence.

Weaver opened the door wider and said, "I think I saw her leave a little bit ago."

"Oh." The policemen looked at the door, then at him. "Okay. I thought she came here, but I'll check at the front desk and try calling her." He nodded to him. "Thanks."

Weaver waited until the man got onto the elevator and went downstairs. Should he knock on the door?

If he didn't try, he wouldn't know, but why would she answer him if she wouldn't answer the other man? The officer seemed to know her.

Still, he couldn't leave it. With his own door closed, he crossed the short distance to hers. The first rap yielded no response. He rapped again. "Paris, it's Weaver."

No response. He looked down the hallway and knocked again. Then he heard the heavy, gut-wrenching sobs within. Shit. Pounding on the door now, he insisted. "Paris, this is Weaver. Let me in."

"No," she cried from inside. "Go away."

"I need to know that you're okay."

"I'm fine," she said, her voice shaking. At the end, it broke, and so did a little bit of the stone around his heart. He'd tried letting his guard down once before in an attempt to lead a normal life. Have a normal marriage. It hadn't worked, so he'd put everything back up thicker and stronger than before. But there was something about Paris that brought it crumbling down again.

"I don't think so."

No answer.

"That policeman was trying to get a hold of you."

She gasped. Suddenly, the door was flung open and she stared at him in shock, her huge eyes terrified. "No, no. He can't find me." Wide-eyed and panicked, she looked down the hallway first one way then the other before grabbing his arm and pulling him inside.

"Why not? Are you running from the law?" he asked carefully. "Or are you just running from him?"

"I'm not running at all," she said crossly, wiping her eyes. "I don't want to see him. Ever."

"He looked harmless. In fact, he looked really earnest.

Like he was hoping to talk to you."

"He's part of my past." Her voice quivered as she shook her head. "I can't see him again."

Wavering on her feet, Paris started shaking.

"Okay, easy." Immediately he reached for her and tugged her into his arms, wondering at this woman who spent so much of her time on his mind or in his arms when what he really wanted was to take her into his bed. The worst thing he could do – for himself and for her. Hell, he'd gone down that path once. So not a good idea. If he was going to be with someone again, it would have to be someone who'd dealt with all her shit. Not someone looking at him to fix her stuff.

As he knew all too well, he couldn't fix anything.

Her body relaxed against him for a long moment, neither of them moving, just resting, needing the peace of the moment. The only sound was their synchronized breathing.

All of a sudden, she pulled back. Never quite letting down her guard. Always aware of that line.

He found it – her – fascinating.

"I'm fine." She walked into the room and sat down on the small chair. "Honest, I am."

"Good. Then let's go get some dinner. I'm starving."

But her head was frantically sending her hair flying out. "No, I can't go down. I might see him."

At a loss for words, he asked. "What if he's here for more than just today?"

A visible shudder wracked down her slender frame. "Then I might just call this week a bad deal and go home."

"Oh boy. Okay, one thing at a time. If we don't want to go to the hotel restaurant and you're afraid to meet up with this person anywhere, I see two choices."

With her arms wrapped tightly around herself, she stared at him hopefully.

"I can either go out and pick us up something or we can order room service."

She blinked at him.

CHAPTER 11

T HE THOUGHT OF pizza made her mouth water, but was there a place anywhere within walking distance? Was it fair to send him? No, it wasn't, and she really didn't give a damn right now. She needed to feel safe. But at the same time…she'd come here to push her boundaries. To get out of that safe world.

But she'd never expected to see that hateful person from her past. Someone who should have represented safety yet only brought up danger in her mind.

And sure enough, her brother's voice rolled through her mind. *Safe is no way to live. We have to experience new things and new people, otherwise our surviving was for nothing. If we choose to live, we must choose to live well, all in. No half measures allowed.* With a big breath, she pushed out the words, "Pizza. I want pizza."

Eyebrows raised, he replied. "Okay, pizza it is. I wonder if we can order one to be delivered here."

"No idea." She walked to the window. Damn it. She shouldn't be crippled by this. With everything she had been through, she should be stronger than that. Who knew Delaney would be here? Or that he'd recognize her? It had been so long and she had changed so much.

She'd grown up.

Or thought she had.

Facing Delaney though would be facing so much more than she could handle right now. She'd come to deal with her issues. But not the one involving him. That was too big. Too painful.

It wasn't possible.

But she might be able to do something. "Look, if we go out through the back of the hotel, I might go. We could slip out for pizza and sneak back in with no one the wiser."

"Like children playing hooky? There are evening sessions we're supposed to do, aren't there?"

Paris nodded. "Every evening there is something going on with Jenna. Although many are one-on-one private sessions with her as she checks in on everyone's progress."

A broken, painful sound escaped. "Right now there is no progress in my corner, just a horrible backward slide."

"And one you can change," he said firmly. "So what if you met someone from your past? He's in the past."

"Obviously not if he's here in my present too," she muttered. "I honestly never expected to see him again."

"That's why the shock then?"

Nodding, her stomach growled making the decision for her, she said, "I'll grab a sweater and we can go."

"If you're sure," he said doubtfully.

With a glare at his lack of support, she retorted. "It's now or never. I won't have the courage to go later."

"Now." He waited while she grabbed her light plum cardigan from the bed and walked out in front of him. "I need my jacket in case of rain again."

She followed him to his room, standing in the doorway while he picked up his jacket from the back of his chair. It was the same layout as hers.

With the hallway still empty but worried she couldn't

get out before that changed, she said, "It's clear. Let's go."

They walked quickly to the elevator and as he was going to push the button, she shook her head. "We'll take the stairs."

USED TO HER sudden requests, he shrugged and followed. Taking the stairs was no guarantee that they would miss the other man. Not when stairs were the healthy option these days. The stairwell was empty at the main floor, but she carried on to the parking garage level and walked out. Wow, she really meant to avoid this guy. Fair enough.

Outside, a light drizzle had started. He stood on the main street and looked both ways. Downtown offered a lot of food options in the daytime, but in the evening it didn't look as promising. "Any idea where to go?"

"There was a place over a couple of blocks. I haven't been there in years, but they used to have good food. Pizza was just one of the choices."

"Good enough." He tucked her arm into his and said, "Which way?"

She pointed left.

The walk was brisk and cool. It was hard to tell if she was walking so fast to escape the hotel or if she was cold and wanted to get where she was going quickly. At least she wasn't looking behind all the time to see if they were being followed. Afraid she was being chased.

Or afraid of being caught.

They were similar but also slightly different, and just different enough to make him ponder her actions.

That it was the policeman she was afraid of made him think she'd been involved in something illegal. Possibly she'd skirted around a crime or seen something. He knew he could speculate endlessly and still not be correct given the myriad of possible circumstances, but he couldn't stop his mind from working the issues.

"What made you go into nursing?" Was that a neutral enough topic to be safe to bring up?

"I love babies."

Good choice, as her voice softened as she answered.

"What's the hardest part of your job?" he asked again, hoping to keep her mind off the scenario back at the hotel.

"Mothers who don't appreciate what they have," she answered shortly.

He glanced over at her in surprise. "I thought it would be the sick babies or the ones that can't be saved, or the disabilities…infant deaths."

She nodded. "Those are all hard to deal with. And there are so many in different situations that you never get used to it as each baby has its own personality. Each mother has her own story, her own personality as well." She shrugged. "In a way, the babies are part of the circle of life. It's terrible and heartbreaking but almost understandable." Her voice hardened as she added, "But the mothers who didn't want their child, or who aren't happy with the sex of their child, or…" Stopping mid-sentence, then her voice quieted. "You get my meaning."

He did. "That's understandable. Especially as it's something you really want and can't have."

"Exactly. It also makes you wonder what kind of life those children are going to have if they are not wanted in the first place."

He peered closer at her, hearing a different note enter her voice. "Is that what happened to you? Were you and your brother not wanted?"

"Who knows?" She shrugged. "Our mother took off when we were little."

"Maybe there was good reason?"

"Sure." Paris gave a short hard laugh. "She was a victim of domestic abuse and was strong enough to get the hell out."

Oh hell. "But not strong enough to take you with her," he guessed.

"Nope. And with her gone, who do you think he turned to next?"

Shit. So much for trying to find a neutral topic.

He squeezed her arm in commiseration and pointed out a fancy old car parked on the other side of the road. Anything to get away from the dangerous memories of her past.

And his.

CHAPTER 12

PARIS WANTED TO laugh. She was outside in Vancouver walking with a very attractive man, about to go and have dinner. Not exactly a date, but better than the guys that belonged to the gang at work going for lunch. It's not that she hadn't been able to date – she'd had lots of opportunities, but she hadn't been able to trust the men. So she'd brushed them off. Good men most likely, but because she was such a basket case, she hadn't been able to take that step. It would have been too difficult to explain any of her problems to them even if she wanted to. Here Weaver already knew she had problems – hell, it was a given in a workshop like this. And he had his own issues to deal with whether he was ready to acknowledge them or not.

That almost put them on equal ground. It removed that big elephant in the room when you went out on a date wondering how much you should explain. *I'm a virgin. I've been abused. I have father issues in the biggest way.* Or the steps that went way beyond that.

I'm terrified of the law. I'm terrified that it made a mistake. That it's waiting for me to screw up so it can get a second shot at me.

None of those were conversational starters. Yet she could likely say that to Weaver.

If he said things like that to her, she wouldn't have a

problem. She understood he probably shouldn't have mentioned the report to her but at the same time, she'd rather know now instead of later. What a betrayal it would've been if he hadn't said anything until later.

And maybe there was more betrayal to come. Anything was possible and she had no idea.

It was almost a given according to Sean. He'd been of the opinion that if you didn't get involved, then you didn't get hurt. At least that was his belief before he'd met Robin. That was funny to remember how much he'd changed. It was seriously a joy to watch how happy her brother was now. And…yes, she was jealous. She loved his partner, and that made it easier. If he'd dropped his sister in favor of a partner, that would have been very difficult for Paris. But he hadn't, and the bonds between the three of them had deepened.

Watching him grow gave her hope, and now her only concern was she didn't want to be left behind.

She wanted a partner too. Or at least know that there was the possibility of one in her life. Weaver wasn't it, and that was okay too, for the most part. He was his own person with his own needs and he had seen too much of her ugly side. He'd also been involved with someone from therapy before and wasn't looking for a repeat of that disaster. That was understandable. Likely it wouldn't be a good choice for her either.

Although it had worked out beautifully for Sean and Robin. Those two were made for each other.

So who the hell was she made for?

"Thoughts? You look so serious right now," he said, walking at her side.

"Just wondering if there is someone special out there for everyone or do some people miss out."

"I think there's more than one someone actually. There's likely to be a different someone depending on our stage of life and what we are looking for. Not all marriages last, and people move on. Not everyone is blessed with longevity, and those that lose a partner often find someone new to love. I think it's just a different love." That made her feel better. "I'd like to experience love once. In some way."

"You mentioned your brother – don't you love him?"

"I really love him," she said in surprise. "He attended a workshop with Jenna a couple of months ago and did phenomenally well out of it. He found someone special during the course. She had as many problems as he did, but they are a perfect match."

"Nice. You don't see that often." His voice sounded doubtful.

"Yeah, you'd have to know my brother to understand how difficult this was for him." She shook her head. "Trusting Robin to the extent he does – it's huge."

"Trusting anyone is huge."

They walked in silence.

"Are you going to tell my why you are avoiding that man?"

Conflicted, she shook her head. "It's not an easy thing."

"Really." He snorted. "What in all of this is easy?" He motioned to the city melding around them. "You left the hotel and came out in spite of him. That wasn't easy and you managed anyway."

She shrugged. "It was almost worse sitting there and waiting for him to come back. I saw him in the lobby earlier and hoped I'd been wrong. In all these years, I hadn't seen him, so why now?"

"If you believe that whole line about everything happens

for a reason…"

"Meaning I'm here at the workshop looking to move ahead and he shows up, so take that as a sign?" She turned to give him a hooded glance. "I had considered that. Then dismissed it."

There was his crooked grin again.

"Too bad life isn't quite so easy to dismiss."

There wasn't an answer to give so she stayed quiet, her arms wrapped tightly around herself.

"He's obviously a huge issue for you," Weaver added.

"Scary huge."

"So maybe see if you can get past it. It seems to me that this week is all about dealing with crap. This crap is what showed up – so deal with it. Maybe look at it as a gift."

"It's too big."

"How big?" he said quietly. "Big enough it impacts your ability to trust. Big enough to impact your ability to move on. Big enough to stop you," he paused for effect, "from moving on?"

He studied her intently. "Because if it is, this is so what you need to deal with right now. Forget the rest of the workshop lessons or what you are trying to make happen this week. This is a golden opportunity."

The thought made her shudder. No way could she handle that one. Not here, not right now. She needed someone to help her through this, not someone to toss her into the river and hope she could swim. As he gently grabbed her elbow and nudged her forward, she realized she'd come to a complete stop in the middle of the sidewalk. And was barely breathing. She gulped for air. And then again. Focusing on her breath and almost subconsciously on his touch, she pushed the panic deep inside.

Before she knew it, she was sitting down on a park bench, Weaver hovering at her side.

"Honestly, Paris, if it's this big…you need to deal with it. It's crippling you."

Tears welled up, and one big fat tear rolled down her cheek. "I know. But it's so big. Such a huge scary thing. I'm always afraid because of him. Always…"

"Then maybe that's what you need to do – face him. Tell him how he has crippled you. Tell him you need him to go away so you can get on with your life."

Her hair flew violently around her head as she shook her head like a dog shaking off water. "You don't understand. This is life-changing. I'll lose my job. My life as I know it will cease to exist."

"WHAT?" WEAVER SAT down beside the distraught woman. "How is that possible?"

"I can't tell you," she cried. "No one can ever know."

"No one?" He was confused and getting seriously worried. This was such a big fear in her life. He could see it was what she needed to deal with. That the opportunity for her was here and now with both Jenna and himself to help her through it. That was something he could do.

"My brother. Sean." She grabbed her cell phone and in between wiping her eyes and sobbing out loud, she sent her brother a text. He didn't want to pry but desperately wanted to know what she was saying. All he could see without obviously reading over her shoulder was *Constable Delaney*.

After hitting send, she slumped back as if that much effort had been too much. Now, looking around, the light lowering on the streets, the wind picking up, he was sorry they hadn't ordered room service. She'd been strong enough to leave but at the same time, they still didn't have food and she looked to be at the end of her rope.

Her cell phone beeped. She swiped across her phone, read the message, and cried out, "Talk to him. Sean, how can you say that?"

Weaver was starting to like the guy already. "It's what you need to do."

"I can't." Cold and dark, her tone of voice said this was a no brainer. She wasn't going there – ever.

She stood up. "I need food, then I need sleep."

And she started walking.

Weaver was lost and trying to catch up as she shifted from the weeping ineffectual woman to this coldly in-control female.

What the hell just happened? And who was the real Paris?

CHAPTER 13

THE BURNING QUESTIONS hung in the cool air around them. Didn't matter. She had no plans to answer them. There were things she could do and things she couldn't do. Talking to Delaney was on the second list. The other constable, whatever his name had been, might be a different story. He'd helped Sean in a way she'd never have been able to reach him. And that had made such a difference to her brother. Sean credited the man with saving him from a deep dark slide into the shadows of his soul and staying there.

But he hadn't had the same effect on her. Watching from the sidelines, covered in blankets but apart from the going-ons, she'd been in shock. And so much of what happened back then was a dim painful memory. To try and look at it closer was asking for a whole lot of pain. Who wanted to scrape their insides out again after it had finally healed? Not her.

Then again, that stupid little voice in her head said, *What if it never healed?*

It had to have healed. It had been over a decade. Surely that was long enough. But that same voice smiled and said, *If it was, you'd have no trouble taking a closer look. Because you won't even contemplate such an action, you know it hasn't. And won't if you can't deal with this stuff.*

"I can't," she snapped.

"What?" Weaver asked by her side.

She flushed then groaned. "Sorry, I was talking to myself."

"Arguing from the sounds of it," he said, his voice light and humorous. "Every time I do that, I lose."

Again she felt his light touch on the small of her back, and her heartbeat quickened. "I can't lose this one," she said resolutely. "It's not possible."

And that was all she was going to say on the topic. The pizza place was one storefront down from them. She hurried inside to get in out of the cold – in more ways than one.

Once back in her hotel room, she answered Sean's text. Her response was clear and simple. "No."

Of all people, he should understand. He'd watched her go to pieces at the time. In a different way than he had. In a different way since, but they'd both picked up the remnants of their life and carried on. It hadn't been easy, but they'd done it and she was always comforted by that fact. What she'd gone through afterwards had been so different than what Sean had gone through. That's where the understanding and mutual experiences diverted.

Her brother knew in theory what she'd been put through, but he hadn't been allowed to be by her side and she'd never been able to tell him. The police had questioned her for hours at the time. The process had damn near killed her. It took months for her to sleep again, afraid the cops were going to come any minute to haul her away. Afraid ever since that they'd made a mistake and someone was going to pick up that old file and remember what she'd done.

Her day of reckoning would come.

She was hell bent on making sure she wasn't the one who had to serve it.

And that meant avoiding all cops, especially the one she'd spoken to back then.

BACK IN HIS room, Weaver hesitated as to whether he should say something to Jenna about the cop being at the hotel and Paris's response. Was it tattling? Or was it in her best interests? He tried to think of it from the therapist's point of view in that he was there to help her heal. If Providence dropped a juicy opportunity like that into his patient's life, wouldn't he want to know?

Wouldn't he need to know? Her behavior was going to be off now – there's no way it couldn't be. And if Jenna didn't know what was going on, she couldn't help Paris deal with it.

The right thing to do was call her.

He opened his cell phone. "I need to meet you. Maybe the coffee shop if it isn't too late."

"Be there in five," she said cheerfully.

That was one thing about her that always blew him away. Not once had he met her in a bad mood. Always wide-awake and cheerful, she was ready to take on whatever the world tossed at her.

He left the hotel room and with a final glance at Paris's closed door, walked down to the coffee shop.

CHAPTER 14

PARIS ANSWERED HER phone. "Hi, Sean."

Silence.

"Are you okay?"

She burst into tears. In between her sobs, she managed to get out, "I'm…" sniffle… "fine."

His voice threaded with gentle loving humor, he said, "You don't sound it."

"Why is he here?" she cried. "Why now?"

"I don't know. Is he there alone?"

"No," she said, her voice rising in alarm, "The hotel is full of cops. Some kind of seminar. Talk about horrible timing."

"And maybe not," he said in that calm way of his. "You don't need to talk to him, but maybe by the end of the week, you could get to the point of not bolting every time you see a policeman."

Her mood lightened. "Well, so far it hasn't worked. I've bolted twice. Once inside to get away and once outside to get further away." She laughed.

"Of course you did." He chuckled. "And you might still do that for a while, but not all cops are bad. Remember that."

"I know he isn't bad. But not all are compassionate and caring. You hit the jackpot there. I didn't."

"No, you didn't, and I've always been so angry about that. I should have been there for you."

"No," she interrupted him. "Don't blame yourself. It's the system. We were victims first, and the system continued to make us victims."

"You more than I. We had a decent foster family for that last while, but they never quite knew how to handle you."

"Without you, I wouldn't have ended up mostly normal." She sighed. "The foster family was good to me. They were a rock when I was the storm. How they put up with me, I don't know."

"Well, it helped a lot that he was a psychologist." Sean's voice deepened. "Did you consider calling him?"

"No, I haven't dumped my problems on him in a long time." In truth, she never had. He'd been great at coaxing her back to the real world, but she'd been a lot of work. He had taken on several other kids after she'd moved out, although she didn't think any were as badly damaged as she'd been.

"Maybe you should let Jenna know."

Silence.

"I don't want to open it up," she said, her voice barely above a whisper. "And she's going to poke and pry and insist that the blood flow to cleanse the wound."

"So? You know it has to happen."

"So," she countered, using his own word. "Doesn't mean it has to happen here and now. Today or this week. It's not what I came for."

"Yes, it is." Again that calm manner and voice that had held him in good stead. "You went there to heal. We don't always get to choose *what* is going to heal."

Paris slumped on her bed and flopped backwards. "It's

too hard to do all of this."

"Sure it is. That's why it's a good idea to bring Jenna on board so that you have the support you need. Think about it, Paris. I know you went with other intentions, but this could be a huge gift. Deal with the cop. See him as the adult you are and not the traumatized young girl you'd been. He won't be the ogre you remember now because you are older and wiser."

"But it wasn't him as much as the power of the law that terrifies me," she reminded him.

"And that's just wrong," his voice rose in anger. "I've told you before. It's not your fault."

Her hand trembled as she brushed her hair off her forehead. Tears once again welled up at the corner of her eyes. "I know you say that…"

"I mean that. Anyone would tell you the same thing. Hell, dozens of people *have* told you the same thing," he said. "It's that asshole sitting at the damn hotel that's to blame for putting that doubt in your head." He made a half-strangled roar in the background. "I'm of a half mind to come down there and beat the crap out of him for what he did to you."

"No," she cried, "you can't."

Sobs broke free, and she couldn't hold them back anymore. "Besides, he didn't do anything other than his job."

"He was a hard ass to you and you didn't deserve it. You were traumatized. You needed support and counseling, not his heavy-handed warnings."

"But he was right. I started down a path and my actions have followed me ever since."

"Damn it, Paris. You escaped your past. You got an education, you got a life. We are both surviving and now I'm thriving. It's your turn."

Sniffling through the tears, she wished he was there to give her a hug. And then unexpectedly, an image of Weaver holding her close crept in, and she pushed it down. "I hope so," she whispered. "But I'm afraid it won't be in time."

"In time for what?" he asked, alarm making his voice rise.

"Before they haul me away."

There was an odd silence. "Why would they do that?" he asked in a low, controlled voice.

"Because he was right," she said, breaking down into heart-wrenching sobs. "I'd do it all over again."

She hung up the phone then threw herself across the bed, lost in the horrible memories of the night she'd killed her father.

THE COFFEE SHOP was mostly empty except for a few cops sitting in the far corner. Jenna wasn't here yet. He took a chair by the window with his back to the wall so he could watch for her. After ordering coffee for two, he waited, unsure if he was doing the right thing.

More cops came in and took a second table a few feet away from them. One was the man who'd knocked on Paris's door. Weaver frowned, wondering if he'd be able to overhear the conversation about to happen with Jenna.

As he looked up, Jenna walked toward him, smiling. As she approached, that one cop stood up and stopped her.

Curious, he tried to listen in, only to realize their voices were so low he couldn't hear what was being said. But they knew each other.

Suspicion settled inside. Had Jenna set this up?

He wouldn't put it past her.

Neither did he believe in coincidences.

These two were up to something. Jenna motioned toward Weaver and the cop nodded. He sat down again and Jenna continued on.

Now he didn't know what to do.

After she'd settled and her beautiful smiling face turned his way, the words spilled out. "Did you plan this?"

She raised an eyebrow. "Plan what?"

He nodded to the cop now busy joking with his friends. "Him."

Turning, she glanced back at the cop then turned to face him.

If he hadn't been watching so closely, he didn't know that he'd have caught it. Confusion, surprise, and maybe a little fear. But not the guilt he was expecting.

She shook her head. "I don't know what you're talking about."

After taking a sip of her coffee, her gaze never leaving his face, she asked, "Explain, please."

Stretching his long legs out in front of him under the table, Weaver sighed. "Paris has gone off the rails because of that man."

"What?" She stared at him, lowered the cup, and leaned forward. "What happened?"

Quickly he explained about finding this man knocking on Paris's door and her refusing to open it. About her crying jag. The escape to the pizza place followed by the little bits and pieces he'd managed to get out of Paris. "She's devastated over this," he finished. "I was hoping she could deal with it now that it's here in front of her, but she's adamant about not going in that direction."

"Of course. It's the shock. The sudden change in plans. When one is afraid, opportunity looks very scary."

She turned to look behind her. Weaver realized the group of men was getting up to leave.

"How do you know him?" Weaver asked.

"Through Child Services. I am working on a difficult case right now. He's part of it."

That made sense. "Maybe that's how he knows Paris."

"Yes, most likely."

"But why would he want to talk to Paris?"

She smiled. "He's seen a lot. If he can, he likes to check in on his old cases and see how they are doing."

"Paris?"

"I don't know." She shrugged and sipped from her steaming mug. "Given her reaction, I'm going to say yes. However, her reaction is not one I've seen or would have expected to see." Her voice lowered as she added, "But in a way… it makes complete sense." She glanced at her watch. "I wonder if she's asleep."

"I doubt she'll sleep again."

Her gaze sharp, assessing, she asked, "Really?"

He nodded "She looked to be heading for a crying jag after we split up."

"That's not a bad thing."

"No, but not an easy one either."

"So what do you want to do?" she asked. "And how is this impacting you?"

Of course she'd turn it around to him. Leaning forward, his eyes narrowed. "I want you to fix this. Especially if you had something to do with bringing the cop here."

"I didn't," she interrupted.

"Good," he said, accepting that for the moment. "Then

help her deal with this. This man is a huge issue in her life. Probably the biggest. If she could find a way to see him, talk to him, see that there's no reason to be afraid..."

Jenna nodded. "Did you consider that there might be a good reason she's afraid?"

No, he hadn't. Sitting back, he stared at her, Paris's weird reactions and her words – had she ever mentioned a reason for her fear? No, he didn't think so.

Still, he just couldn't believe she'd be guilty of anything. He shook his head. She so wasn't the kind.

"Remember," she said, her gaze gentle, her voice serious. "Under duress, each and every one of us is capable of doing the most horrible things."

CHAPTER 15

T HE NEXT MORNING, Paris dragged herself from bed and straight into the shower. She didn't look in the mirror. She already knew how her face was going to look. The heat and tightness said volumes on their own. She stood under the pounding water and let it sluice down her face.

She'd barely gotten any sleep. Nightmare after nightmare dragged her up from the depths, only for her to fall under again from exhaustion. Now there was just exhaustion. This must be what it was like to live in hell. No. She already knew what hell was like.

There was another text from her brother waiting for her when she got out.

Did you think about it?

"Think about what?" she wondered aloud. But she knew. And she had thought about it. About the pain that cop had caused her. The fear she'd carried since forever. The nightmares he alone was responsible for.

Why would she be willing to talk to him?

Especially now.

As she looked at her first days at the workshop, she couldn't believe how much time had gone by and how little progress she'd made. The reason she'd come was to see something measurable. Something she could look back on and see the progress. She needed to see progress. Healing.

Inside it felt like she was doing the opposite.

That made her mad.

Why should this man pop into her life and destroy her like this? It wasn't fair. She'd been doing her best. Crossing her t's, dotting her i's for a long time, making sure there was never a reason for anyone in law enforcement to doubt her straight and narrow path.

And look what she got. The return of the one cop who'd destroyed her peace of mind since that lousy night. Before that night, there'd been a lot of lousy nights. A continuous stream of them. They'd been the norm.

She was an adult now. Not a child. Not a teen. Not a destroyed girl waiting for the good things in life to show up. For years she'd believed they would, then she grew older and she'd given up on them showing up. Now as an adult, she realized they *were* all there. One just had to look for them. And one couldn't focus on what was there before or else the bad things completely eclipsed the good things and redefined what 'good' things meant.

Like now.

Dry-eyed and tired, she sat wrapped in a towel on the end of her bed and wondered how she was going to get through the rest of this week.

She'd wanted to come since forever. Now she couldn't wait to go home to the point of considering that she should leave early.

Sad, drained of hope, she realized she wasn't going to find her miracle here.

WEAVER KNOCKED ON Paris's door, hoping to coax her down to the restaurant for breakfast. No answer. Feeling foolish, he knocked several more times. But she either wasn't there or wasn't planning on getting up anytime soon.

"Paris," he called out gently, "I'm going to the restaurant. Why don't you meet me down there?"

And he left. As he walked to the elevator, he turned to check to make sure she didn't open the door. But it stayed closed. After his talk with Jenna last night, he'd been feeling a little guilty. He was suspicious by nature, and Jenna's words had kept him up for hours last night.

Had Paris done something wrong? Was that why she was so afraid? He couldn't see it himself, but who knew what someone did? Especially a long time ago. She'd been abused. That much he knew. How long and how badly were details he could wish for but didn't see himself getting.

Taking the stairs helped him clear his mind before walking into the restaurant. As it had been busy last night, he half expected to see it the same way this morning. No, of course not. It was empty. He was early.

Maybe that's why Paris wasn't up. He took his usual seat and ordered coffee and opened his menu. Pancakes and eggs would be a great way to start the day. Closing the menu, he stared out the window. As he watched the few people rush by, he realized a long lean woman sat on a bench at the tiny corner garden. Damn it. That was Paris.

She sat so still, like a stone, he wondered how long she'd been there. She had to be cold. She wore a long gray sweater and had it wrapped around her, her fingers clutching the material together at the front as she stared at the flowers in front of her. He doubted she saw any of the beauty. Finally, she moved, standing up to stretch. Holding his breath, he waited, hoping she'd turn so he could wave at her. Instead, she sat back down in a different position.

Damn. His coffee arrived just then. He stared at it. Then at her.

Making a sudden decision, he called the waitress over and asked for a takeout cup for his coffee and a second one to go for Paris. Within minutes, he was striding out to the tiny city lot and the kaleidoscope of colors growing in the rough environment. Kinda like Paris.

She never heard him coming.

"Paris?"

Her back straightened and then slowly, as if afraid of who called her, she turned around. As her gaze landed on him, she smiled.

He grinned back, relief washing through him, his heart warming. At least it wasn't him she'd been trying to avoid. That it mattered should have worried him. Instead, he brushed it off as just concern for her. It was just part of the workshop, he told himself. She was struggling and he could help.

That he admired and respected her was normal. She was valiantly trying to find her way on a road that had shown her more rocks than flowers so far.

That she might help him never occurred to him – or rather it slipped in and out of his mind just as fast. This was not about him. He'd come out here to see if there was something he could do to help her.

"Here, you look like you could use this."

Her smile brightened as she accepted the cup. "Thanks."

"You're up early."

"Couldn't sleep."

"I hear you there." He sat down on the stone bench beside her. "It's another day, whether good or bad."

She snorted. "I spent my life saying bright and happy

things to cheer myself up. They weren't working this morning."

Weaver nodded, studying her. "Understandable. It takes time after a shock."

"Yeah, that's true. Time. Like lots of it."

There was an odd note in her voice.

"You don't sound like you're doing all that well this morning."

"Sure I am. Just had a difficult decision to make."

He waited, then curiosity got the better of him. "Oh? What decision?"

"Whether I stay and finish the week or check out this morning."

CHAPTER 16

S O MUCH FOR keeping that decision to herself. Telling him would just give him a chance to talk her out of it. Then again, maybe that's what she wanted. To be talked out of her decision. She didn't know anymore. She'd cried buckets this last day and she was so done with that. She'd never been a milksop, and just the thought of someone thinking of her as weak made her mad.

Waiting for him to tell her not to, she stiffened her back and her resolve. This was the right thing to do. Crawl away and come back another day. Sure, Jenna might not do a different workshop, and that would have to be okay, too. There were other people that could help her. Other people were skilled and caring. Jenna was right the first time when she let Sean in and not Paris. Paris wasn't ready. Not back then and maybe not now. Sad but true.

She realized that Weaver hadn't said a word. She slid a sideways glance his way, studying him as he studied his coffee. She traced his strong features visually before closing her eyes with a sigh. There was an urgency boiling up inside her, and in this confused state, she did not know how or why it involved him, but it was there. Waiting for her…

"You haven't said anything."

He looked up in surprise. "No. It's your choice. But I just realized I'm going to miss you."

His words shocked her. From the look on his face, his words shocked him, too. And that surprised her even more. Caring was something he obviously guarded against, and he hadn't recognized the sensation for what it was.

For her, the problem was she often cared too much and had been hoping to knock some of that back. Everyone at work always confided in her, told her their problems, looking for help in finding a way forward.

Here, she'd been the one with the problems. Weaver had helped her through the days. Only she didn't want to mistake gratitude for something else. He mattered too.

"I'll take that as a compliment," she said.

He was still staring at her in surprise. So much surprise it was almost insulting. "Am I that bad that you're so shocked to be missing me?" Her attempt at a light tone failed, her voice cracking with emotion.

Damn it. He could take that look off his face any time.

"No." He shook his head, a lopsided grin sliding out. "Not at all. But I didn't expect to get to know anyone here, and certainly not someone that fascinated me."

"Right, that damn report." She frowned. "Another reason to leave. I won't be in your report."

"You weren't going to be in it anyway," he said absently. Her breath sucked in. The shock and surprise he expressed had changed to an internal contemplation, or at least that's what she thought the distant inward look in his eyes meant. Hell, she didn't know anything about this man, so she shouldn't be making any assumptions where he was concerned. Still, he was a nice guy. Nicer now than at the beginning of the seminar. And warm, and sexy, and she so shouldn't be noticing. Except there was something appealing about that self-confidence. That hidden vulnerability she wasn't sure he was even aware of. But it was there. That he cared was a bonus. Hell, what was she talking about – it was a huge bonus. She liked him – a lot.

Before she went any further, she stood up and said, "I need food."

"About time." He bounded to his feet. "I was in the restaurant when I saw you out here."

"Ah," she teased. "So you're just trying to get me to go inside so you can eat."

"I could have eaten before," he said with a smile. "Still, it's much nicer to eat with someone else." He reached out a hand for her to take. "Like you."

She stared at it. It was likely the first time a man had done that. Why had he? Why now? And if she took his hand, was it a commitment? Because it sure felt like it.

WEAVER REACHED OUT and clasped her hand. She'd taken so long to decide he took the choice away from her. His ego could only stand so much. No one had ever called him an expert in women by any means, but he knew enough to know she was interested, or would be if this whole mess hadn't blown up in their faces. They'd had a rough beginning and then a rough middle. But when they touched, he could feel their warmth mingling into something new, something exciting. He figured if he could get her to stay for the rest of the week, they might have something worth trying to connect with after that.

But in order for that to happen, she had to take a few steps towards him. And he wasn't sure she could do that on her own.

Holding his hand could be construed as one of those and

proved his point.

Together, they walked back to the restaurant. Every once in a while, he caught her looking at their joined hands. Smiling, he used his other hand to push a strand of hair behind her ear. "Never held hands with a man before?"

When she didn't answer, he glanced over at her to see a rising tide of color on her neck and face.

"Actually, no," she replied, the honest pain evident in her quiet words. And still she held on.

CHAPTER 17

P ARIS FELT THE fool. Her own innate sense of honesty said she had to answer the question, but it felt odd. Just as odd as holding his hand. The heat from his much larger one surprised her. The firm, muscled pad. Large, lean fingers that dwarfed her own much smaller ones. Even his body radiated a warmth she hadn't expected. She was always cold. Inside and out. She thought it was that she was so skinny. And maybe it was, but he obviously had no problems there. Then, he too was lean, muscled.

She sighed.

"And more heavy sighs." He laughed, and damn if the sound wasn't carefree and young.

"Glad you're in a good mood." She looked at his laughing mouth and slid a little closer to him, wishing that sense of freedom would rub off.

"Hey, I'm walking with a pretty girl and heading for breakfast, my favorite meal of the day," he said with a lazy smile. "What's not to be happy about?"

"Men are so simple," she said, but she felt better. Lighter. Just a few words of acceptance. Of being wanted. Nice.

At the restaurant, he led her back to the same table where they'd sat before. "Order what you want," he said, "I'll be back in a few minutes."

As he headed to the men's room, she watched his long

easy strides. She'd have bet money that he was smiling. The waitress arrived with menus, so she ordered coffee for both of them.

"He's a cutie," the waitress said with a big grin. "As soon as he saw you outside this morning, he hopped up and grabbed the coffees and went right over."

The waitress left, but the envy in her voice had Paris smiling. Nice to think someone was jealous of her. Her own feelings toward Weaver were mixed. And confused. But definitely interested.

Maybe she didn't understand what she was feeling. This was new and it was something she hadn't ever felt it before…

Weaver represented something she didn't comprehend as she'd never been down this pathway before. He was also something she wanted. It was nice he was interested, but would he still be if he knew everything? Probably not. How could he? He'd said he was friends with a lot of cops. That meant he was okay with law enforcement and all they symbolize.

But he was also waiting for Justice.

Another sigh escaped her lips. She was too in many ways.

And she had nothing against cops in general. It was just this one.

The waitress walked back and deposited two cups of coffee on the table before walking away again. Paris barely noticed, lost as she was in her thoughts.

Weaver was right. This cop was the huge problem in her world. She stirred her coffee, staring in the depths, realizing something else she'd forgotten. Sean had been good at reminding her of small truths. Something he'd said a week ago stuck with her. He said, *Giving away your power made you powerless in the face of adversity. Call back your power so at least you are on equal footing.*

She *had* given away her power to this man.

He was just a man. He'd only ever been just a man.

She was the one who'd given him the elevated status of being the *bogey*man.

Having the force of the law behind him added to the effect. What she'd been through lent more power to it. She'd already been victimized. Thinking back, she realized she let herself be victimized ever since.

Not fair.

Weaver sat down in front of her. He reached over and clasped his hand over hers. That was when she realized she'd been stirring her black coffee – something that didn't need stirring – with enough force to make it slop up the sides of the cup. In fact, the saucer was full, too.

She sat back and stared at him. "I gave away my power."

His gaze widened, but he stayed quiet as if giving her comment due thought. Then he gave a clipped nod. "In a way, yes."

She dropped her gaze to the table. "It's a weird feeling looking back."

"Hindsight always is."

She laughed, but there was no humor in the sound. "It's also painful."

The waitress arrived to take their orders, but the mood had been broken. Paris didn't want to bring up the subject again. Though maybe she should speak to Jenna about it.

"Do me a favor," Weaver asked when the waitress left. "Before you check out, talk to Jenna first."

"Oh." She frowned. "I hadn't thought of that."

"She gave you a spot in the workshop, handpicked you

for this, I suppose you might say. I think she'd appreciate the respect of hearing it from you firsthand."

Paris grimaced. That wouldn't go down well. Still, she'd subconsciously made the decision to stay but hadn't realized it until he brought it up.

"That would be the right thing to do."

"Yeah, it would," she said. "I will speak with her."

Satisfied, he sat back, looking pleased with himself. As if he believed Jenna would be able to talk her out of leaving, and true enough, she likely would. "I already decided to not leave the workshop."

Delight lit up his face, and damn it if that didn't warm her heart, filled some of the cold empty places inside. Maybe he really did care. She grinned, the weight on her chest easing. It was time for something good to happen in her life. Maybe he was the right one after all. Did she dare hope?

"Why?" he asked. "What made you change your mind?"

"You for one. It's nice to know I'm not totally alone in this. That you'd miss me. Thanks for that. My intuitive flash about having given away my power. Jenna – there's no way I'd want to have to tell her I wasn't strong enough to stay," she say wryly. "That woman is something else."

Weaver laughed and laughed. "Good reasons." He leaned forward, holding her hand firmly but gently in his. "Honestly, I wouldn't want to tell her either."

Just then their food arrived and they dug in, having moved on to a new step in their relationship.

WEAVER WONDERED AT the lightness inside. That sense of relief at her words. Why should he care so much? She was a stranger, really. But a fascinating one. And he was intrigued and attracted. Sure, some of it was professional, but a lot of it wasn't. It was like seeing an animal in pain and he might just be able to help her. She might hate him for it. This could end with her moving on like his wife had done. Afterwards, she might want nothing to do with him, seeing him only as a painful reminder. He'd helped his wife through a very difficult time and she'd been grateful – but then he'd become part of her negative memories and she needed to move past that.

He sighed. That was his garbage. Not hers and not Paris's.

"And here I thought you were happy. Instead, you're sounding depressed all of a sudden," she said, her gaze intense.

Their eyes met. He wondered if she felt insecure inside and afraid of having read a person wrong. If so…well, it was something he could relate to. Leaning back against the bench seat in a relaxed slump, she looked more at peace. Weaver pondered how far they had come. There were bags under her eyes and her skin missed that wonderful vitality of a good night's sleep, and yet she wasn't self-conscious. Or wary. It all seemed to have melted away.

He smiled gently at her. "I'm very happy. And I am proud of you," he admitted, seeing the flash of surprise in her eyes before she had a chance to cover it up.

"Wow, you're easily impressed," she mocked. "I was in the process of running away."

"But you didn't," he reminded her. "And that's huge."

Her laughter was light and genuine. Then she glanced at her watch and said, "We're going to be late if we don't get moving."

They stood up, paid the bill, and walked over toward the

conference room. As they walked past the elevator, the doors opened to let half a dozen men exit. Law enforcement officers.

She gasped, averted her face, and picked up the pace.

They were going in the opposite direction so the men passed them without even seeing her. Weaver couldn't see the man she was trying to avoid.

Still, she didn't run. Reaching up, he put a comforting hand on her shoulder and squeezed. Leaning into his touch, she tossed him a thankful grin back.

And damn if he didn't seem to need that as much as she did.

CHAPTER 18

PARIS WALKED INTO the seminar and took her seat. Her insides were still shaking but as the incident had come and gone so fast without any kerfuffle, she felt like she'd just been spared a major confrontation. Now if her breathing would just calm down, she'd be fine.

Jenna arrived within minutes, and boy did she have a stack of paperwork in front of her. She smiled at the group at large.

"Homework," she said, holding the stack up amidst the outcry of groans. "Not hard, but thought-provoking. I want you to spend much of this evening thinking about your life, your past. Especially your future. Remember the questionnaire you answered on the first day? This moves forward based on the answers you gave back then. I'm going to hand those back to you, and you're going to use that one to help you fill out the second one."

Jenna ignored the groans erupting from the room. "Both are due back first thing in the morning."

One person piped up in the front, "That's a lot of homework, are we going to be given any time to work on it during the seminar?"

"No." Jenna shook her head. "But we will be doing intense thought-provoking workshops to help you start the process. It's important that you drop all the baggage you can from your life so that you can start as fresh and as powerful as possible as you move on to the next stage."

"What next stage?"

Paris didn't see who spoke. She was still remembering the paper she'd ripped to shreds and the piece she'd actually eaten. Lord, she wasn't going there. Yet, already her stomach heaved at the thought of someone seeing it.

"And are these answers going to be made public?"

Jenna shook her head. "They will be given to me only. This is, as always, confidential. Everything that happens in these seminars, the work you do, the stuff I see – it belongs between us – and only us."

There were a few nods, a couple of heavy sighs. And then silence as people waited for her to continue.

"So I'm going to hand these out later. Break into groups and get started."

Paris hated the group work, knowing it often triggered deep stuff publicly. So far it hadn't been that way, but the further they got into the workshop, the more likely it was to happen. Already she felt like she'd been through the spin cycle of a washing machine this morning. That meant her defenses were already low. Being tired made her more vulnerable than ever. Then there was the reminder of her first worksheet too.

It didn't forecast much good about the coming morning.

In fact, the morning was even worse than she feared. By the time the lunch break rolled around, Paris was exhausted. Dragging her tired, worn-out body upstairs, she headed for her hotel room. This day could not end fast enough. The delightful breakfast she had shared with Weaver seemed like ages ago. It wasn't that the exercises had been hard. Or that they had been intense. But it was difficult to listen to so many people deal with their own garbage. And in this scenario, the exercise amplified everyone's problems. There had been a lot of tears. A lot of breakdowns. A lot of hugs.

The surprise for Paris had been that there was no breakdown for her. But she was so weary. She needed some downtime – especially after no sleep last night – some time to distance from the emotional waves of energy.

Unlocking her door, Paris stepped into her hotel room. Without thinking about it, she set her keys on the desk and flattened out on her bed. She was asleep within minutes.

When she woke, disoriented, she had no concept of time. A knock sounded on her door. Weaver's voice called from the other side of the door. "Paris, are you okay? It's late. The afternoon session is due to start in a few minutes."

"Sorry, I fell asleep." She opened the door while still rubbing the sleep out of her eyes.

"Don't be sorry. You were exhausted." Weaver hesitated at the doorway.

Her heart still pounded, her skin clammy. She reached over and flicked on the light, blinking at the brightness. "I'll be just a few minutes. Go on ahead without me."

"Are you sure?" he asked.

She nodded firmly as she closed the door.

In the bathroom she washed her face, taking only a quick glance at the mirror. No change. Still the same tired, flat Paris that arrived here days ago.

A few minutes later, she walked into the restaurant and asked for a coffee to go. There were muffins on the back wall. Thinking of her own stomach and Weaver's, she ordered two to take with her. The waitress grinned and said, "Your boyfriend was just here. He ordered the same, only he had two coffees to go with it."

Boyfriend? Nice thought. A long ways from the truth, but a nice thought.

Paris thanked her and walked away with her goodies, feeling ashamed. Had Weaver bought her a coffee and a muffin? She could share her muffins, had in fact, planned on it, but she hadn't thought to buy him a coffee. Thinking in twos had never before been necessary before.

In the seminar room, sure enough, he waited with a coffee for her. She sat down beside him and shook her bag of muffins. "Sorry, I didn't bring you a coffee."

He laughed. "Not an issue. I could use a second muffin, and I'm sure you can use a second coffee."

With a big grin, she replied. "True enough."

"Class," Jenna said, walking in just then. "We have a long hard afternoon as we're going to do the prep work on the worksheets now. So get into the groups you started with this morning and we're going to mix things up a bit."

Paris groaned but obediently shifted to the table on the far side. Jenna didn't like anyone working with the same group of people all the time. Her theory was that the comfort level became a hindrance. Paris didn't agree, but it didn't matter what she was thinking here. Jenna was the boss.

Still, it was rough. In the middle of the afternoon, Jenna walked by, handing out the worksheets. The ones they'd already filled out was stapled to the back so no one could see the answers but the owner of the papers. Paris did a quick check and winced. Yeah, that was hers all right. It had a big rip in the page and multiple folds from Weaver's origami. She hastily folded the paper and tucked it into her purse. If it was homework, then she'd do it later tonight. There was no way she was going to answer any questions on her old sheet's condition. As she glanced at the new homework sheet, she realized it had nothing to do with the old torn set of questions.

Weaver stared at her, one eyebrow raised.

"It's all good." She gave him a bright smile. He hadn't said anything, and she appreciated it. At the same time, she doubted he'd let her off the hook completely.

Just as the afternoon appeared endless from an emotional session where several people in her latest group had broken down and Paris knew she was on the verge of tears herself—the subject matter this afternoon being mothers—as if that wasn't enough to trigger something for everyone, there was a knock at the door. Expecting to see a hotel employee, she couldn't hold back the shocked gasp at the sight of Constable Barry Delaney.

Immediately, she hunkered down in her chair, her panicked gaze darting around the room looking for an escape. But there was only one way in or out. Unless she used the window. Panicked, she actually considered it for a long moment.

"Jenna," the constable asked, "Can I have a few minutes of your time?"

Jenna walked closer. "Sure. This session is almost done, then I have about an hour free."

"Perfect."

Jenna turned to the group. "You have your homework, so you're good to go for the evening. Those of you that are scheduled to meet with me tonight, please be prompt. The schedule is tight. The first appointment is in an hour, so please don't be late. There is time for dinner if you don't mind eating early. Other than that, I'll see you all tomorrow. Remember, worksheets are due first thing in the morning."

She walked to her desk and started to sort papers.

Chaos ensued throughout the room as everyone stood up to leave. Several small groups of people stood around discussing the latest of the projects while others formed, making plans for the evening.

Paris froze, her mind scrambling for an escape.

Weaver stood up and walked around so he was between the cop and her. "Come on."

In a blind panic, she shook her head vigorously. "He'll see me," she hissed, darting a look toward the doorway.

The constable wasn't looking her way, but he was gazing at the attendees as they packed up. Shit. He'd see her in a few minutes. There was no way he wouldn't.

"Not if you sneak out in the middle of the group," Weaver said calmly. "He hasn't seen you yet, so chances are he won't if we keep people between you and him."

"I'm scared," she whispered, clutching her purse against her chest, her fingers white as they gripped the leather.

"I know, but you're going to have to face him sooner or later. Better sooner."

"Better never," she muttered.

"Come on, let me help you out of here."

She stared at him, uncomprehending. Then got it. He was going to help her escape. Quickly scrambling to her feet, and seeing a half dozen people heading for the door, she realized that now was her chance. Keeping her head down, with Weaver between her and the cop, she raced toward the doorway.

Weaver grabbed her hand and stopped her headlong rush. With his calming presence, she made it to the door. The cop had moved out of the way as the group headed toward him. She was in the hallway in seconds, sweat pouring down her back, her breath locked in her chest.

When she reached a point about six feet past him, she snuck a look behind her.

Delaney wasn't even looking her way.

Shuddering, she leaned into Weaver and let her pent up breath out. Oh Lord. She'd made it. She'd also caught a close up look of the man who'd brought her nightmares for the last decade. His face looked older. Sad maybe. Like he'd seen too much of life. She could emphasize. She had too.

She wished she had a chance to study his face without him knowing. So she could replace the childhood memory with the up-to-date one. Surely that would help. But then as if sensing her glance, he turned her way.

More relaxed now that they were out of the room, Weaver's grip had loosened. Up ahead she saw the stairwell and before either of the men had a chance to register her actions, she'd bolted up the stairs.

WEAVER FELT HER hand slip away, but she moved so fast he didn't have time to react until she was gone. He watched her take the stairs two at a time as she ran away. Should he go after her?

"Weaver."

Jenna's voice called out to him. Reluctantly, he turned and walked back to her. She was in conversation with the cop that Paris was trying to avoid.

Smiling as usual, she made the introductions. "This is Constable Barry Delaney. He specializes in cases with children at risk."

Weaver studied the man with interest. There was a calm steady look to the man. He reached out and shook his hand.

"I was hoping you could help me talk to Paris," the constable said. "I've been hoping for a chance since I saw her here. I can see she trusts you and I…" He stopped and shrugged. "I have a little unfinished business with her that I'd like to clear up."

Weaver didn't know what to say. Did he help Barry or did he help Paris? Were the issues one and the same? He didn't know. At a loss, he turned to Jenna. She stared at him, completely neutral. Really? Was she testing him somehow? He wanted to glare at her but knew that wasn't going to help.

The man seemed earnest, but the bottom line was simple. "Paris doesn't want to see you."

The man's shoulders deflated. Rubbing his face roughly with his hand, he nodded. "Understandable. I said something to her that I'd thought was appropriate at the time, but her words and reactions have eaten at me. I misjudged her then. I didn't know the extent of what she'd just been through. I was new to the department and had just come on to the case." He stared at the empty space between Jenna and Weaver, his gaze unfocused, distant. "When I learned the details, it was too late. She refused to talk to me again, and I never got a chance to fix it. I can't take back what I said…"

Forcing a smile, he continued. "I had hoped she'd moved on and done well for herself, but when I saw her here and she ran from me, I realized I had to clear the air."

Shit. Weaver stared at the man who appeared to be earnest and caring. If his words had hurt Paris unintentionally, then that was likely what Paris's issue with him was all about. She definitely needed to see him. But Weaver knew if he pushed it, she would hate him.

Yet, it was holding her back right now from having a full life.

Really shitty timing.

He glanced over at Jenna and this time, maybe she'd seen the change in his own stance. Maybe she'd been on that side since the beginning. But there was a decidedly positive look in her eyes as if to say, *You can do this, Weaver.*

It was true that he could, but he also felt like he was betraying Paris. How did he reconcile that?

He sighed. "What do you want me to do?"

CHAPTER 19

PARIS STARED UP at the ceiling. She had her phone out and had already tried to call her brother several times. So far he hadn't answered even though she really needed him to.

Things were crashing here and her foundation was slipping. This was huge and when she said huge, she meant *huge*. Too huge. She couldn't handle it. But she just knew it was going to require handling.

That truth hit her stomach and came back up – with her coffee and muffin from lunch. She bolted for the bathroom and just made it as her stomach emptied.

On the floor, tears in her eyes, hating herself for hitting this point, she could feel herself unravel.

Somewhere along the way she should have grown up. She should have found a way to deal with this years ago. Not here and now when she was looking to move on. Moving on meant going forward, not dealing with these huge chains around her soul holding her back – well it did – but she hadn't realized how big and cumbersome the chains where. How ingrained the hurt was into her psyche. And if she couldn't walk through a doorway and see a person without puking up her lunch, they were bigger than she realized.

That bothered her more than anything.

Had she been so blind to not see the effect this man had

on her every action? Had she just been so accustomed to her own reactions that they'd been commonplace and 'part' of her? So that nothing looked or felt different enough to be noticeable. Had this man's words controlled her reactions since? If they had that much power back then, how much effect had they had on her since? When she hadn't even realized they were there, like little marionette strings yanking her chain all these years.

Was she so weak? No. She wasn't.

Was she so powerless? No. Not now.

Was she so incapable of moving past this she couldn't function? At the moment…yes.

And that couldn't continue. What had happened, had happened a long time ago. She'd done the best she could in a really shitty situation. Where survival had been the goal. Her brother had survived. She had survived.

Her father had not.

It was her fault, and at the same time it wasn't her fault.

Her own fear had brought her down this pathway. Her survival instincts had been right on. She'd been traumatized, then the cop had traumatized her more.

Now her own future was dependent on her accepting this. Not just accepting, but acknowledging her actions. By saving her brother's life and her own, she had to live with the consequences of her actions. Only she hadn't.

Trying to build a life. Trying to get through each day without letting her history define her present and not affect her future.

But what about the cop's words? Said in warning. Taken as a threat. She'd internalized his words and held them up as the one fight she still had to win. Yet did she? Still?

All these years. She was still living with a victim's mentality.

Had she made no progress at all?

Dry-eyed now, she stared down the long history of her life. At the damage her childhood had on her. The impact her actions had played in her life. The effect the others around her had on her then, and now.

Being a victim, in her case, had meant not showing any kind of reaction, just locking everything inside. In her early years, she learned quickly that to show a reaction was to take a beating if she showed the wrong one at the wrong time. Her father never left clues as to what was right or wrong, and she'd been beaten regularly. She'd always gotten back up. In fact, it had been a point of pride. Maybe not at the time, like Sean had, but later after the danger had passed. She'd gotten up again and carried on.

She thought she'd grown out of it, changed her attitude, and become stronger. Now as she considered how she'd let the constable impact her life, she realized she was – at least in his case – still in victim mode.

In many areas she had moved forward. After going to school, she had a good career and loved her work and the people she worked with. Always went when called in. Always stayed late when needed. Always worked hard. Not because she wanted to but because she was afraid not to.

Sadly, still in victim mode, still afraid of the consequences of saying the wrong thing. Of saying "no."

Truly she'd gotten nowhere. All of the goals and dreams she had, and yet she hadn't taken the steps to fulfill them. She hadn't put in an application for adoption because she was sure she would not be accepted. Nor had she tried relationships because she was sure it would go bad. If she didn't try, she didn't fail. But maybe that was because the right person hadn't come along yet.

Weaver was here and interested – she didn't even know how interested because she hadn't given him that opening. Every corner of her life, she held back just in case she did it wrong and got beat back down. Instead of living, she was waiting for the other shoe to drop, waiting for something to go wrong.

Victim mode.

WEAVER FELT LIKE he was betraying Paris. "I don't want to do anything that will make her feel ganged up on," he said to Jenna and Delaney. Jenna had been mostly quiet through this exchange, but he had a strong sense that she wanted his help. That it was fine to help, but they might not understand the long-term impact this man had on Paris.

"No, of course not," Jenna said. "We'd like her to be happy to meet Barry, but if that isn't going to happen, we need to give him a chance to say what he needs to say to her before she runs. Maybe then she'll have time to process the words."

His head was already shaking. "She's going to run as soon as she sees him. There's no way she won't."

Jenna frowned, and then turned her head to see if maybe Paris had come up behind her. "I'll talk to her."

"Good," Weaver said. "You do that. I'm all for helping her, but not for hurting her."

"And you know she has a lot of hurt to go through to get to the help?" Jenna watched him, as if looking for a chink in that armor of his.

Nodding, he felt defensive. "She's already had a lot of hurt, and I don't even know the full story. I don't want her to feel betrayed by us and have all that hurt magnified.”

Constable Delaney spoke up. “I had no idea I hurt her that badly.” He looked devastated.

As much as he wouldn’t mind letting the man suffer for all the fear Paris had been through these last many years, he couldn’t let the man suffer more as well. “It’s a combination I think. There was a lot going on before you and whatever you did compounded it.” He shrugged. “I’d love to know the history of this but as she won’t tell me, I’m kind of in the dark here.”

“And it’s not my confidence to share.”

Jenna looked over at Barry. “Let me talk to her first. See if I can get her to see reason here.”

With a sad look, the constable nodded and turned away. “Make sure you tell her that I don’t want to hurt her. I never wanted to hurt her. I just want to apologize.”

And he left, heading in the direction of the restaurant and bar. If Weaver were a betting man, he would put his money on the bar.

“Thank you, Weaver.”

Startled, it took a couple seconds for Jenna’s words to soak in. “Thanks for what? I didn’t exactly agree to your plan.”

She smiled again, and damn, he was going to lose himself in the depth and compassion in her eyes if he wasn’t careful and he forgot his focus. “You did what was right for you. That’s all we can ask of anyone.” Her gaze intensified. “How are you doing this week?”

He thought about it. “I don’t know. I’m a bit lost actual-ly. The seminar is what, half over? Almost half over and I haven’t written the report on the workshop or even started the project in the workshop.”

"Life isn't just about the academic side of things. There are a lot of emotions flying around here. How are you handling that?"

"Trying to stay separate and detached is difficult," he admitted. "I don't know how you manage it. I'm not sure I could do something like this."

"You don't have to." She laughed. "There are many fields where your expertise and input would be welcome."

"Well, I don't feel that I have any expertise," he said, "and I haven't had much to input anywhere yet." That note of chagrin in his voice had her grin deepening.

"Yes, the joys of being a student. We know everything one minute and we know nothing the next."

"Exactly."

"How are you getting along with Paris?"

That question slid in so smoothly he'd already reacted before he could answer. And he knew that sharp gaze of hers caught every nuance. He decided to be honest. "I'm getting along fine with her. She fascinates me," he admitted. "She's so strong and in control one moment then so broken in the next. She has amazing defenses in place, and if Delaney hadn't shown up, it's quite likely she'd have blazed through this workshop without a dent to that cool, blasé control she shows to the outside world."

"Yet you see inside?"

He nodded. "I'm seeing inside. Just not sure I'm seeing very *far* inside. She's very complex," he said in what he hoped was a neutral tone of voice. At her knowing look, he realized he'd failed. A tide of color washed up his neck.

"It's not like that."

She nodded, but her smile didn't dim. "Good."

Already looking for the elevator, he stopped and said,

"Good?"

"Well, if it's not like that, then you won't toy with her affections."

He blinked. "Sorry?"

"If it were like that, then you'd be interested and she might be interested back. As you're not interested, then she won't get hurt more."

Blinking again, he stepped toward her. "Am I missing something?"

She shrugged. "I don't know. Are you?"

"Damn it, Jenna," he snapped. "Don't play games."

"I'm not. You just said you're not interested."

"No, I didn't. I said it's not like that," he corrected. "*She's* not interested."

Now she gave him a fat smile. "You need glasses. You don't seem to be seeing too clearly."

Then she walked past him to the restaurant. He stood there and stared at her in bewilderment. Was Paris interested? He had been getting mixed vibes from her all week. Then she was a huge mix of all emotions. He didn't think it was very healthy to start a relationship under these conditions.

Then he stopped once again. And groaned.

Hell, one way or another, he was already in a relationship with her.

CHAPTER 20

Paris knew what she wanted to do. But she wasn't sure she could. She had to think about it carefully. Failure was not an option. There were many times in her life she'd said something similar, but this time she knew the consequences would be horrific.

But she'd always been a survivor.

She had to take the chance. Had to.

Right?

No. It was a choice, but one she needed to make.

God, this was going to destroy her. She flopped backwards on the bed once again, confused and upset. Torn. What she thought and felt seemed to change every few minutes. She was an idiot who couldn't even make up her own mind on what to do. How to do this.

The conference was wearing her down. She knew it was deliberate on Jenna's part. They started with little exercises to take the top layer off, leaving everyone feeling a little exposed. A little vulnerable. Then they started digging at the newly exposed tissue, trying to open another level of pain. Of hurt.

Her stomach growled, putting her focus on more mundane issues.

Damn, lunch had been a long time ago.

She glanced over at the clock. It was almost seven. Was

her one-on-one session with Jenna tonight? She couldn't remember if it was. No. If so, she'd cancel. Postpone it. Panic once again rose at the thought of meeting Jenna. Another layer, or ten, would be ripped away. Something that was supposed to happen, but the pain and fear she was going through right now was excruciating. And then there was the panic. That immediate response to the stressor that said, *No. Run. Hide.*

Shuddering, she climbed further into the blankets and buried her face.

Someone knocked on the door. She froze. Was it the cop? She leaned over to make sure she'd locked the door, then she curled up in a tiny ball and just rocked herself gently on the bed. Whoever it was, they'd go away. Soon. Surely.

Instead, she heard Weaver's voice. "Paris, open the door. I brought dinner."

In a low voice, she protested. "What if I'm not hungry?"

But she was. She was starved. And Weaver wouldn't give up as easily as another man. He didn't look like he had much give in him at all.

"Open up, Paris. It's Greek."

"What if I don't like Greek?" she called out as she walked toward the door, wiping her eyes, knowing she looked a mess. Well, that should send him away if nothing else. But she really liked the guy. Knew he liked her, but there wasn't any way they would get together. At least not permanently. She was good with that. And having Weaver in her room would be a distraction. His warm laugh, piercing eyes and muscular physique would be a welcome change to the gnawing uncertainty that wracked her thoughts.

She opened the door to see Weaver, wearing an aura of

concern, standing and holding a large takeout bag of Greek food. His muscles bunched as he held the bag, and he frowned when he saw her. It made her smile.

Maybe she wasn't good with that.

"You're making me crazy," she said, pushing the door open wider and letting him in. Turning back inside, she tried to calm the rolling emotions in her head, stomach, and damn it – her heart. She didn't want to care about him. She didn't want to care about anyone. She'd be opening herself to a world of hurt. And him with his lopsided grin and light-hearted manner, what if it was all a game to him? A fleeting thing. She didn't know that she could do that.

She really just wanted to do what she wanted to do and forget the rest. *Liar,* her head whispered. *You want what Sean has. You want someone special. You want to see where the warmth of his touch will take you.*

He's not special though. He's arrogant, rude, ignorant and…caring, compassionate, sexy as all hell and…so very nice to look at.

She groaned. "You really are going to make me nuts."

"I'm making you crazy? I haven't done anything to you," he protested, following her inside. "What are you talking about?"

"Oh, nothing," she said with a snort. "One minute you're looking gorgeous and happy and the next you act like a gargoyle, then you're back to looking gorgeous again," she said crossly.

"WHAT?" HE DIDN'T know what to say, and his mind went from gargoyle to gorgeous. Did those two words even belong in the same sentence? He couldn't see it. "Gargoyle?"

She snorted. "What is it about men that they pick up on a single word like that?"

Walking to the small coffee table that sat in front of her couch, he set the bag of food down. "You'd rather I ask about gorgeous?" he asked dryly. He sat down beside her, watching as she worked efficiently without asking him about it, dividing up the food onto two plates and handing him one.

Without a word she took her seat, picked up her plate, and proceeded to eat with a vengeance.

He ate much slower, keeping an eye on her, noting the red eyes and the pale cheeks, the hair that was brushed back off her face impatiently several times. "You worked up an appetite?"

Her glare would have melted glass if there'd been any heat behind it. He laughed. "Okay, so a tough afternoon, but we're here, eating, and that's good, right?"

She shrugged and kept eating.

Not knowing what to say, he was still stunned at her gargoyle and gorgeous comment. Had Jenna been right? Did she like him? Was she interested in him? Damn, he felt like a school kid again trying to sort out matters of the heart. He'd been much older when he learned there was no understanding them.

Now he was right back to being confused. He sighed and stared down at the delicious Greek potatoes on his plate. His appetite was gone. Why was she suddenly so important to him? This last outburst from her seemed so open and honest, and heat rose within him.

"Don't you like it?" she asked in between bites, eyeing his still half-full plate.

"Are you trying to steal my food?" he asked mischievously.

Smirking, she said in a crafty voice, "If you give it to me, I'm not technically stealing it." Putting down her own empty plate, she waited expectantly.

"Wow." He split the rest of his meal in half and pushed one half onto her plate. She snatched it up and settled back to eat again.

"How can you eat so much?"

"Nerves," she said. "Always been high-strung."

"I can see that. You're very slim." Weaver replied, looking her up and down.

"Add boyish, slim as a board, pancake. It's okay, I've heard it all."

He raised his head and said mildly, "I wasn't thinking in terms of your chest size."

"Good thing as I don't have one." She smirked and popped a big chunk of potato into her mouth. "The nice thing is I can run without those things flying in my face, too." And damn if she didn't make a comical face that had him shouting with laughter.

Another side of her he hadn't seen before. If she could laugh at her physical body, maybe she'd get to the point where she could laugh at her other problems too. It was great to see.

"See, I knew I could bring out the other side of you." She picked up another bite.

"What other side of me?" As her words had mirrored his thoughts, he was confused for a moment. "What are you talking about?"

"You're too serious," she said. "You rarely laugh. And never at yourself."

"How would you know?"

She grinned. "As I do it all the time, I recognize it in others – or the lack of it."

"Maybe I'm just not comfortable enough around you to do that."

"Maybe," she said cheerfully. "And maybe you're just not comfortable around yourself."

Damn.

CHAPTER 21

WHERE HAD THIS great mood come from? But saying what she wanted to Weaver without fear of repercussion was huge. So freeing. Having him here in her room, felt comfortable, and so much more…

"I'm really glad I can say anything to you. It's given me such a sense of freedom."

He nodded, but there was a distance to his gaze, as if he'd turned inward. And he likely had.

Still, she polished off the last of her meal. "Thanks for dinner by the way."

He slowly reached over and put his plate down on the coffee table then sat back. He said, "Care to clarify that comment about gorgeous and gargoyle?"

With her eyebrows raised, she said, "Hell no. Figure it out yourself."

"I was working on it. Just not sure where you were going with it. See, I really like you. I'd love to see you when this week is over. Maybe go to a movie, have a pizza, and take it to the beach," he said with a light shrug. "Take it slow. Nothing too pressuring."

"What if I want pressure?" she asked, her words shocking both of them. Instantly, she could feel her blood pounding in her veins as she sat breathless for a second. Who the hell was this talking? Surely it wasn't her. Fear had always stopped her from being so open, so… flirty.

He sat up and tilted his eye sideways as he assessed her closer. "Meaning?"

"There's that academic side of you, looking for answers." Paris avoided his question, not really knowing the answer herself. Wanting to touch him, to feel him touch her as they shared their innermost secrets with each other, washing themselves of their past. Shaking her head, she looked up.

"And there's that side of you that darts forward, drops a bomb, and then retreats in case it blows up and you're caught in the backlash."

"Oh," she said in a small voice. "Does that make me a tease?"

This time it was his eyebrows that shot up. "If you do it sexually as an advance and retreat, yes, that would make you a tease." He shrugged. "I wasn't seeing or saying that. I'm seeing more of a baby deer darting forward in life excited and carefree but gets out a little too far and remembers mother's warning so it dashes back to safety." Now his voice was warm and caring again.

"Nice. I think I like that analogy. Except the mother part," she added, thinking of her own mother. "You'd have to have a mother who cared enough to warn you. I barely remember mine. She walked out a long time ago."

"Ever tried to look for her?"

Her headshake was so violent her hair flew out in all directions. "No. And can't see myself ever wanting to." Besides, she'd be tempted to punish the woman like she'd been punished. And that wasn't going to end well.

For anyone.

The joyous lightness inside dropped as she contemplated her mother and her instinctive response to his question.

Maybe that damn constable had been right after all. What did that say about her?

"Hey, why so serious? I'm sorry I brought up your mother." Leaning forward, he placed a gentle hand on her leg.

She watched his fingers close around her kneecap and squeeze gently. A man's touch that wasn't out to cause pain or humiliation. How about that?

If she sat there much longer, she might just ask him to take her to bed and prove all men weren't assholes when they had a woman vulnerable in their grasp.

But so not the way to have a relationship. As an experiment yes, relationship not.

At the word experiment, she froze. That's what he'd been doing in this class. Right.

"Am I an experiment for you?" she said before she let herself double question the sensibility of asking. "Cause I don't think I could stand that." She scrambled to her feet.

"What?" he asked, shaking his head as if to question her sudden switch in conversation. "No. Hell no."

She glared at him. "Damn well better not be."

Walking closer, not sure what she was going to do herself, she leaned over and…kissed him.

SHOCKED AND A little overwhelmed at the suddenness of her actions, Weaver was afraid to respond in case she bolted. He didn't mind being an experiment for her but would prefer to understand exactly where he stood in this study. Not that she'd let him know. As she eased back, a gentle sigh on her lips, he leaned forward, following her retreat.

"My turn," he whispered and tugged her onto his lap.

She made a startled sound, but he covered her mouth with his own and teased her lips open for him. Smooth and dark, he deepened the kiss until she sagged in his arms. He lifted his head, wondering at the shakiness inside himself.

With her head against his shoulder, she whispered, "Nice."

He grinned. Finally they had found something they agreed upon.

CHAPTER 22

ACTUALLY VERY NICE, but she didn't want to make too big a deal over a kiss. Except…it was a big deal. She'd been kissed before. Even in ardor, but it hadn't done anything for her. She'd participated to see if it was something she *could* do.

She could. Just why would she? Previously, she hadn't felt anything. It had been wet and sweaty and awkward and hell no. It was not something she had wanted to repeat.

For her partner at the time, well, they'd been friends and that had been more of a *hey, we've gone out a time or two it's past time for a goodbye kiss.* For her, it had just ended that whole sex thing.

After all, why do it if it didn't feel good?

Now Weaver's kiss – yeah, that had felt good. Dry and warm and caressing, his kiss had made her feel cosseted, safe, cared for. He'd been compassionate, yet there'd been heat under there. A banked heat that also said he was in control. And it left her wanting more…

Like she'd said, "Nice."

And now what? Did she just lie here and wait? Wait for what?

"Glad you think so," he said, humor lacing his voice. "I thought it was nice too."

Lifting her head, she gazed at him suspiciously. His

smile deepened.

"Are you laughing at me?" she accused him, pushing up to look up at his face.

His grin widened and he snatched her back into his arms. "Absolutely not."

"Hmm." Then he lowered his head, and damn if she didn't reach up to meet him halfway.

So this was what you were supposed to feel? She wanted to analyze the sensations but his hands stroked across her back, her shoulders, distracting her. The gentleness of his touch, the soothing stroke so unlike anything she was used to. The warmth flowed between them, erasing all the hurt of the day, melting them together.

When he lifted his head the second time, she curled up against his chest, closed her eyes, and relaxed.

It had been a tough couple of days. There was a feeling that the seminar was over – almost over – a winding down in some regards. The workshops had been helpful. She'd seen a few of her problems. She just didn't know how to deal with the big one in her face.

What was she supposed to do with that?

Usually she'd call Sean and talk it over but ever since he'd hooked up with Robin, she'd tried to give him more space. If he could be there for her, he would. She almost wanted him to swing by. Maybe stand by her side while she pondered the possibility of seeing Constable Delaney.

Delaney. A coldness whispered through her. He'd become a blockage she couldn't get around. He was an issue that she *had* to get past. So far she'd managed to avoid him, but she knew that wasn't the answer.

If only she could figure out how to go about it.

Neither did she want to turn around to find him standing there. She needed to be prepared for the confrontation.

"Thoughts?"

The sound of his voice rumbled up his chest under her ear.

With a pained voice, she said, "I'm thinking about the cop I'm avoiding."

"Hmmm." Non-judgmental, listening, waiting. Nice.

"I know I should face him, but I don't want to."

"Sometimes we have to do what we don't want to do," he said. "And often what we think is a huge deal before and turns out to be nothing afterwards. We can see it had only been big in our minds. Is this man likely to hurt you today? No. It's still the child in you that sees him as a big bogey-man."

"I don't know," she said, her voice barely audible. "I might still be a child when I see him, in my mind at least, but the fear is real." Her chest tightened. "The panic is there, the inability to breathe."

"Right. To be expected. Even now at the thought of talking to him, your mind is recreating the same panic it had when you were a little girl. Although you realize he's not going to hurt you, or haul you away, or any other number of ugly scenarios, your mind doesn't want to let go. It's too locked onto that belief."

Abruptly, she pulled away from him. He held her back for a moment then reluctantly let her go.

"It's just really hard." There was a long pause as she stared at him, considering his words.

"Yes, it absolutely is." He waited a moment then admitted, "But it's so worth doing. This man is crippling you. He's stopping you from being the person you want to be. From having the life you want to live. Is that what you want?

Is that who you want to be?"

Shaking his head, he continued before she could protest. "I haven't known you for very long, but I already know that's not what you want for yourself. Not what you want to be able to tell your kids down the road when you've recovered even further and look back on this stage."

"That doesn't make it all doable though." She settled sideways on his lap, hating that her breath was still hiccupping in her chest and her blood flowed too quickly in her veins.

"Everything is doable. Just in small doses." He grinned. "Kinda like that worksheet."

She frowned at him. "What worksheet?"

"The one from the first day...the one you tried to erase then ripped, balled up, and finally ended up swallowing."

The memory of her chaotic panic had her scrunching up her face in disgust. Though she had come a long ways since then.

He laughed and pulled her close to him again.

"Oh, *that* worksheet," she muttered.

"Are you ready to tell me what the answer was that you felt so strongly about?"

She shook her head violently. "No."

LEANING BACK, IT was his turn to sigh as he tried to not let the disappointment choke him. He knew it was about trust. Another big issue for her.

Maybe one she could handle and maybe not. Maybe if he took the first step...shared something he kept private...

After all, he had his own issues. Lord did he have issues.

"My father was murdered," he said suddenly.

She gasped and spun around to face him, "What?" she cried. "When? How?"

Hating his own instinctive physical withdrawal that happened anytime he remembered that incident in his life, he just stared at her. "I don't normally tell anyone that." In fact, he wasn't sure when was the last time he brought it up. The sympathetic looks and sideways glances people gave made him uncomfortable, made the situation worse.

"Wait...I thought you'd been abused as a child?"

He could understand the confusion in her voice, her words. "After my father was killed, my mother fell to pieces. She took to the bottle. But along with the bottle came the rage, the sorrow, and the complete inability to deal with life ever after."

"She's the one who beat you."

He nodded. "For being home late. For being home early. For not getting up on time. Because the dishes weren't done. Because she didn't have any money. Because she didn't have a bottle in her hand." Wondering at the ease with which he spoke, he shrugged. It was easy to talk to Paris, especially with her so close. "I think the alcohol let her release the rage about my father's untimely death in a way she couldn't do sober. She was always apologetic afterwards, but then she was never sober anymore so there were never any breaks when she was nice."

"Is she still alive?"

He nodded. "She's been in and out of rehab for a while now. It got really bad until I grew up enough to fight back. The trick is to fight back just enough but not do any damage or the cops look at you like you've done something wrong."

Frozen in shock, she stared at him and finally managed to strangle out, "That's very true." Several times her mouth opened and always closed as if to add something, only she couldn't get the words out.

Curious, he waited for her to speak.

Finally, she gave up. Then out of the blue she said, "I'm sorry for your mother and you." She looked at him, "How did your father die?"

"It was stupid. It was a carjacking and my dad resisted. He was slammed to the ground and stomped on before the assailants took off in our car. My mom and I were standing on the side of the road while it happened. We'd done what we were told to do. He, on the other hand, had loved that car. He hadn't wanted to give it up so easily."

"And they killed him?" She gasped.

"Yes, he had internal bleeding in the brain. It was hours before he got medical attention and the doctors did their best, but he didn't make it. I was six at the time and he was only thirty. My mom a couple of years younger."

"Ouch, that's tough."

He shrugged. "Everyone's got tough stories. Sometimes we can get past them and for others...it takes time."

"And for some people, it's never over. Instead, it becomes a living, breathing thing inside, ready to flare up. Ready to demolish your hard won calm and make you realize that, in fact, nothing has changed."

"I know that feeling too," he said. "After my mother spent months at a time drunk, it was tough to see any point in surviving. I had nowhere to go. At ten, I'd thought of running away, but where would I go? I had no other family. Didn't have many friends, because living with a drunk keeps those numbers down. Hell, I couldn't have friends over and hadn't had a birthday celebration or party since losing my father. My life didn't fit the same life other kids were living.

Then again, I wasn't living. I was surviving.

"The killers were never caught. Are not likely to ever be caught." After all these years, he still felt an ache in his heart. "The police figure the man who actually did the damage was part of a gang. Chances are good he's never going to pay for what he did."

"I'm so sorry."

"Like Jenna said, Justice is an issue for me. There's a big part of me that wants to make that asshole pay. And another part of me that says I need to just move on. Move forward and let it go. But saying that and doing that are two different things."

CHAPTER 23

PARIS STARED AT him. They were so different. For him, Justice was something he wanted, and she was afraid Justice wanted her.

She slipped off his lap and moved over to the chair on the side. It wasn't that she wanted to put any distance between them…but she wanted to put distance between them. This was getting intense quickly.

"That must have been difficult growing up," she said quietly.

For long seconds he was silent, then he opened up a little more. "For years, I hated my father. Hated him for dying. Hated that he'd been more concerned about his car than his family, but I've come to understand. I doubt he was thinking at all at the time. He likely just reacted and paid a high price for his resistance."

"I'll say," she said with feeling, hating what he'd been through. "And your mother, did she blame him too?"

"Absolutely. That made it harder for me. As she was so angry, it was hard not to get angry at him as well. She was a good woman. One who, once she slid into the dark side of life, could never get back to the right side again."

"That's very sad," Paris said. In his eyes, she saw the sadness of a little boy who had been through unthinkable tragedy.

"The trouble with any kind of dependency is it becomes a crutch. She could always find forgetfulness in a bottle. The anger came when there was no bottle and reality slapped her in the face."

"I imagine those scenes would have been tough."

Her father never drank. Said it made fools of men. And he was no fool. No one and nothing was going to have that type of control over him. Never. He was bigger and better than that and always would be. But inside, he was a raging ball of anger with extreme hated of his own father and he despised his mother. But his uncle, just mention that man's name and her father went ballistic. Her father had been one scary dude.

It was years later when she heard him muttering about the kiddy pedophile uncle of his that she realized her father had likely been a victim, too.

This was the first time in a long time she had thought about these things. She'd forgotten a lot of family history lessons in life, probably on purpose. The ones she remembered hadn't been pleasant. Of her mother's family, she knew nothing. Maybe she never would. Now though she no longer hated her mother for leaving them. It was highly likely that she had been abused as well. Too bad she hadn't taken her children with her when she finally escaped. Paris's childhood would have been very different if she had.

"Life is a bitch sometimes," Paris said.

"Yes it is, but when you hang around with people in therapy, you realize we all have stories to tell but many of us don't want to share. Why would we?" He shrugged. "We've already lived through it. We just want to move on."

"Do you feel you've dealt with it all, or do you give Jenna a pat answer to those uncomfortable questions, knowing inside that you're lying?"

He gave a bark of laughter. "You do that too, do you?"

"Absolutely. I figure she must know."

Nodding, he continued solemnly. "I think I've dealt with a lot of stuff, but I'm still struggling in some ways."

"Such as…"

"Jenna thinks I should go see my mother." He winced. "I haven't seen her in ten years."

"That's a long time to go without a mother." She should know. Would she want to meet hers after all this time? Or would she just be angry – even now?

"Not really. It's hard to look her in the face and accept that my life sucked in a big way because of her."

"Interesting. Any remorse for her? Sadness? Any hope she'd make a better life for herself?"

"Sure, but I don't want to be involved in the process. I haven't forgiven her. Better to just let her be and see if she's strong enough to get out of the cage she built herself."

"But cold for her and maybe lonely for you?"

He gazed off into the distance. "Loneliness is an issue for people like us, isn't it? Before we can share, we have to know our secrets will be safe. Otherwise, we can't really be our-selves, and the trouble is compounded when you hook up with someone going through therapy too. Your partner will be dealing with their own stuff and that can be just as difficult."

"Was that the problem with your wife?"

"Something like that. She desperately wanted to get mar-ried. To not be alone. But once married, it took her only a few months to figure it's what she'd needed but no longer what she wanted. If that makes any sense. I'm still trying to sort my way through it all. And likely will never get an answer." His voice had taken on a weary tone, as if he'd trashed this one to the end and back and still had no idea.

"Do you still see her?"

He shook his head. "No," he said. "She moved back east to be closer to her family." Then, rolling his eyes, he explained, "She said something about how I'm part of her past and she didn't want to be reminded of me and our short life together so it was better this way."

Paris laughed. "Too bad she didn't figure that out before the nuptials."

"So true." He grinned. "Still, it's nice to be able to laugh now, but at the time…"

"Everything hurts when it happens."

"That's for sure." Looking over at Paris, he smiled. "I do tend to avoid women with baggage. So many have issues."

"No," she snickered, "you're looking at this all wrong." Her smile widened. "You're actually seeing women who are trying to deal with their shit, instead of women who aren't even acknowledging it *is* shit!"

His laughter rolled free before dying away to a comfortable silence.

Now what? She didn't know how to proceed. What to say? But she did feel like she knew him a lot better. Liked him a lot better and felt closer to him. Her mind wandered back to that kiss. Maybe too much so.

Certainly he had been through a lot in life.

Why the hell had Jenna put them together again? And that brought up the damn report. She stood up again, intent on walking to the window. He held out his hand. Letting him tug her back down onto his lap, she tried for nonchalance and asked, "So how do we take all this and turn it into a visual project for Jenna?"

HAPPY TO HAVE her back in his arms, he tried to focus on her question. Visual? Interesting directive from Jenna. He wasn't a painter or artist of any kind, but there was one thing he'd done a lot of over the years. He asked her, "Can you paint or do some kind of art?"

Paris gave a quick headshake. "I do stick men."

"Good to know." He laughed. "Well, maybe we'll have to cut magazine pictures and create a collage of some kind."

At the look of surprise on her face, he realized she likely hadn't done anything like that. Like him, she'd had a poor childhood. School would have been an escape if she'd had a way to stay there after hours. It certainly had been that way for him.

But maybe that hadn't been an option for her. If her father had demanded she return right at the end of the school day, then she wouldn't have gone against that.

Once he'd grown too big for his mother to hit, life had changed for him. He'd done whatever he wanted to do and whenever. Not that the change had been a good thing, and it certainly hadn't stopped the abuse. Just the physical beatings. In a way, he'd almost become the parent in that relationship.

Paris hadn't had that choice. She'd been younger and with her father being the abuser, well, it would have been damn hard to have protected herself from him.

Weaver would love to show her life wasn't always so hard. That there were good people in it. She had been through school and nursing training. Most of the time she related well to people, but there was that inherit lack of trust with men specifically. Big men. Understood. But he was gentle. Or at least he could be gentle if that was required. And in this case, it was definitely required.

Holding her in his arms, he kissed her gently, thinking about the simplicity of the moment in contrast to the complex reality of their lives. It would be easy to stay cocooned with one another. His eyes drifted over to the bed and he took a breath.

How to proceed? Because he really wanted to spend time with her. Sex was one thing, but this…this could be so much more.

But she had to want it as much as he did, and she wasn't even close.

CHAPTER 24

"**W**E'RE SUCH A mess."

That shot his eyebrows into his hairline. "I *was* a mess. Sometimes I'm still a mess, but lots of times, I'd like to think I have my crap together, thank you very much."

Lifting her head, she smiled. "You're also very nice."

Kissing her upturned forehead, he tilted his head in acknowledgment. "Thank you. I like you too."

Snuggling in closer, she dropped her head onto his shoulder and nuzzled his neck. "Would you like to go to bed?"

Instead of getting a laugh or shocking him, he froze.

This time, it was her turn to see if he had stopped breathing there for a moment. A kind of hiccup escaped his lips, then he answered, "I'd love to go to bed."

And he didn't say any more.

So had he meant to go back to sleep? In which case, was she keeping him up? She pulled back and looked at him warily. "Does that mean you're sleepy? Or..."

He grinned. "Or..."

Her cheeks flushed with heat and she turned to look out the window. "Ha." Wishing she'd kept her big mouth shut, she backtracked quickly. "We're strangers. Aren't you supposed to do that with someone you love?"

His eyebrows shot way up. "Really. How about someone

you like a lot? Someone you're interested in getting to know better. Someone you might like to spend a lot of time with."

Her cheeks were hot, but her gaze was steady as she stared at him, still snuggled close to him, their hearts beating in unison, the heat rising between them.

"Your big issue is trust," he said, looking at her with big eyes.

She dropped her gaze and slowly nodded. "I've never really been interested in anyone before. So it hasn't really come up. I'm essentially a novice, and that's always intimidating."

A laugh lit up his face. "It's also reassuring."

She frowned at him, loving the lighthearted laughter in his voice, and wanting to be able to make the move her body was urging her to, she asked. "Why does every guy want to be the first?"

"I couldn't care less." He shrugged. "It's just nice to know that you don't spend all your time hopping in and out of men's beds."

"What if it was women's beds?" she teased.

"There is something almost appealing about that."

She laughed. "Men are so simple. Sex, sex, and sex."

"Hey, this is the first time the subject has come up between us. We've known each other a whole three to four days."

Instantly she gasped and said, "Oh my, that's right. That's so not long enough."

"Not long enough for what?" he cried in a mock-pitiful voice. "If it's right, it's right, and time doesn't come into it."

"I'm not holding out for the church wedding and white picket fence, remember." She smiled. "I'm actually looking to adopt as a single parent. I didn't write men off, just thought it wasn't likely to happen to me."

He tugged her upward into his arms and lowered his mouth to hers. Kissing her gently but thoroughly, his hands stroked her back before reaching around to hug her close. When he lifted his head, it was her pulling him back in for more. Breathless, they looked at each other.

In a voice deep and low, he said, "Well, maybe you should rethink that."

THE CONFUSED CLOUDINESS in her gaze was a total come on. He'd done that to her. And although it was arrogant of him, he was also damn happy he'd been the man to put it there. All he could think about was her. He wanted her more every minute. A mix of confusing sides, she was hard to read. How she'd survived was beyond him, but she had, and she was sweet and caring and had so much to give. He could see that she'd poured all that love into her patients. Those lucky babies. And given the strength and power of love, he couldn't help but think those babies must have responded beautifully.

He lowered his head again and closed his eyes, gently savoring the sweetness of her lips. The tenderness of her touch, the softness of her hair. The acceptance as she lay in his arms. He'd had several relationships. His own childhood abuse, not having had a sexual content to it, had geared him more to being disdainful of women. Tarring them all with the same brush. But he could never see this woman the same way. There is no way she would turn to the bottle to forget or abuse a child because she was so full of anger.

Paris had spent years working to heal. Trying so hard to adapt. To be strong and to survive. She'd done it at great cost – emotionally and spiritually. But she'd done it, and that was important.

She wasn't like his wife. And he had to remember that.

Paris was her own person, and she'd be damned if she'd allow anyone to compare her to someone else.

Good thing – he didn't want anyone else.

Just her.

CHAPTER 25

THE TASTE AND touch of his kiss…the feeling of those strong fingers slowly rubbing her back, exploring her ribs and caressing her skin. Nice. Addictive. She'd always wondered. Always wanted to have someone to hold her. Especially after seeing Robin with her brother. Seeing the affection and caring, how love bound them together.

And it had started here.

Like her relationship.

Was it possible? Could miracles hit twice in the same location? Third time if they counted Robin's friend Tania. And maybe more. Jenna's workshops were legendary. Who knew how many relationships started with them? And she had to wonder how many lasted.

This wasn't about having a forever perfection – although like every woman, she certainly wanted such a thing if it existed. But she'd take little bits and pieces of wonderful goodness for now. Weaver was extraordinarily kind. He'd been looking out for her in the same way Sean had done for decades. Maybe that was the attraction. But it was more than that, it was his touch, his smell, the way he would not back down but was gentle at the same time. It gave her hope.

"What are you thinking?" Weaver asked, the heat of his breath sliding down her cheek to her neck as he trailed a line of kisses across her face.

"You remind me of my brother," she said honestly, tilting her head to give him better access.

He froze, lifted his head, and said, "I don't feel brotherly toward you."

And this time when he kissed her, it was as if he wanted to erase the thought from her mind, stamping his personality on her soul, taking possession of her needs and wants and spiking them higher and higher.

Heat coursed through her, feelings she'd never experienced before making her shiver – with want, with expectation, with need. She'd missed out on this in life. It felt so good. So right. She wanted to see where it could go.

Wrapping her arms around his neck and pressing closer, she was willing to see what more there was. What more he could show her. Make her feel and forget. To enjoy this moment.

He shuddered then shifted and she found herself lying flat on the couch beneath him.

The weight of him on top felt so natural, so good. She loved the rapid thud of his heartbeat. The red flush on his neck and face. The glitter to his eyes. She wasn't scared of him.

And though it shocked her, she trusted him.

With a sexy smile, she murmured as she placed tiny kisses at the corner of his mouth, "Take me to bed, Weaver."

WEAVER DROPPED HIS forehead to rest on hers. He closed his eyes. He wanted this. He really wanted this. But he needed to know she was okay with it – regardless of her words. Or maybe in spite of it.

He opened his mouth, and she placed a finger against his

lips, telling him to stop.

"Don't ask if I'm sure. I'm sure. Don't ask if this is what I want. It's what I want. I know this pushes my boundaries and yours. But I can do this. I want to do this. Besides…"

The little catch in her voice was barely audible but he heard as she added, "Besides, I trust you."

His heart overflowed. For many guys, they wouldn't care about that. For him, it was major.

"Thank you," he whispered. Slipping off the couch, he grinned at her wide-eyed confusion. "No, you didn't say anything wrong." He held out his hand. "I figured the bed would be a whole lot more comfortable."

With a startled laugh, she stood up with him, already walking backwards to the edge of the bed, his gaze intent, searching. He wanted her to be there inside – right there with him – and maybe she was, but he was going to give her every chance to back off if she needed to.

It might kill him…but she needed to be in control. At the edge of the bed, he flicked off his shirt and tossed it back on the couch then unbuckled his belt while slipping off his shoes. Seeing her gaze widen, he leaned forward to kiss her. She shook her head and stayed just out of reach.

Uncertain, he watched her retreat. Only she grabbed her own shirt and pulled it over her head and tossed it onto the couch with his. With a bark of laughter and sheer joy, he quickly divested himself of the rest of his clothing.

He stood in front of her, nude, aroused, and comfortable in his skin, waiting, watching as she did the same, matching him step by step.

When they were only a foot apart, both nude, she swayed toward him. He tugged her close, feeling her shock as heated skin met hot skin. God, he wanted her. His need was something he couldn't hide. Lord was she beautiful. Long, lean, muscled, but gently rounded everywhere.

"Are you—"

Her mouth latched onto his, silencing him as she began to explore his body.

Yeah, he'd have to say…she was sure.

CHAPTER 26

SHE'D BEEN SHOCKED at the sight of his aroused body. Not at the physiology of an aroused man. Anyone with access to the Internet got more than they ever wanted to see there. No, her shock was at the proof that he wanted her. Something she'd never expected to see.

Briefly she considered that when he saw her rib and hipbones sticking out, he'd be turned off. Instead, there'd been a stronger reaction, as if he was pleased with what he saw. Like go figure.

Then he'd opened his mouth, and she'd wanted to stop the question again from coming up. Maybe she didn't want to be given a choice. To be given a second chance to wonder. To doubt.

It wasn't that she *needed* to do this. There'd been so much in life she'd needed to do – just to survive, to function in that crazy world of life after being a victim.

This she *wanted* to do for herself.

Clumsily, she'd kissed him, trying to express the feeling roiling through her. And again, he hadn't seemed to notice her lack of experience or her roughness. He was so damn accepting and so damn sexy, she wanted to explore, to touch every inch of his body.

And she loved that he seemed to authentically care about her. For the first time, she realized how far she'd come this week. Who'd have thought she'd be standing here with him right now?

As he pulled back slightly, she didn't let him go.

That same lopsided grin came out and chased the worry away. "Just a minute," he whispered.

He stepped around her, grabbed the bedding, and pulled it down to the end of the bed. Then while she was still figuring out what she was supposed to do, she was scooped up into the air, a tiny shriek escaping, and tossed into the middle of the white sheets. The cold bedding hit her skin, making her gasp, only to have that sensation followed by his long muscled body coming down on top of her to chase away the chill. In fact, she was now surrounded by an inferno. Inside and out.

Her body woke up in a big way. In a way she'd never known was possible, but she'd gone from being slightly cool, slightly uncomfortable, to being hot and twisting beneath him, wanting so much more.

She knew the mechanics but hadn't expected the emotion. The heat or…the overwhelming need and the connection, the power of touch.

Lowering his head, he proceeded to show her all she'd been missing. And she let him. Acquiescing, she followed where he led and he didn't disappoint. A whole new world of experience opened up for her.

As he stroked her ribs and kissed the old scars she'd completely forgotten about, her hands felt their way along his broad shoulders. His fingers stroked and caressed her small plump breasts before taking the nipple into his mouth and suckling. She arched her back in surprise, wondrous at the surge of sensation not only at her breast but between her legs. This was almost pain…yet so pleasurable it was a feeling she did not want to end. She was so confused and over-whelmed as he caressed and explored, awaking nerve endings she never knew existed.

When he slid two fingers into the curls at the juncture of her thighs, she cried out in joy, almost weeping as pleasure washed through her.

"You're so responsive," he whispered, kissing her navel and licking his way below, past the long scar and multiple little ones.

She twisted and cried, whimpering when his tongue slid over her nub, her body open and desperate for release. Lifting her hips, she tossed her head and gripped him with her body. Her fingers dragged through the dark curls on his head. She didn't know if she wanted to pull him up to her or push him lower. She couldn't think – just feel.

Then he slid lower.

And he tasted her, licking her as if she was the best ice cream cone. When he slid two fingers deep inside, she cried out, her hips arching up and away from his maddening touch.

Until something twisted inside her.

He grabbed her hips, held her down, withdrew his fingers, then slid his fingers in again.

She exploded.

A kaleidoscope of colors matched the rolling waves of sensations driving through her body. She'd whimper if she could. She'd laugh in joy if she could. Instead, she could only lie there and shudder.

Waves upon waves of…joy washed over her, around her. She was in the center of the vortex. Sensations so freeing and wonderful she just lay still in delight and let it happen.

Weaver kissed his way back up, stopping to taste her

navel, her nipples, before giving her a deep drugging kiss that pushed her deeper into the center of the vortex. It was barely noticeable when he shifted her position, making a place for himself, like he belonged there.

He lifted her hips and in one sure stroke settled himself deep inside her core.

Gasping, her pelvis, with a mind of its own, softened. Accepting, caring, welcoming him, reaching up for him.

There was no pain. Just a newness. A sense of rightness.

She sighed. How could anyone stand this? It felt so good. So *right*. So full. So much more than she'd ever thought it could be. It was…perfect.

Then he started to move.

And she realized it was happening all over again. The pressure built up quickly, and she couldn't do anything as the sensations buffeted her from one side to the other. It was going so fast, all she could do was hang on for the ride.

She opened her eyes to see him, his own eyes closed, the cords on his neck tight and hard as he drove toward something only he could see.

Then he gave a long groan, his body arching backwards, and she could feel his release inside her. So deep inside. So special. With him in a togetherness she did not know was possible. And damn if she didn't come apart again.

He collapsed beside her, their bodies slick with sweat, and he tucked her up close. She lay curled up at his side, wide-eyed yet exhausted. Her body hummed. Her emotions spun and her mind…it couldn't believe what she'd just experienced.

No wonder everyone spent so much time thinking about sex. Where to get it, how to get it, having it, and who with. Holy crap.

She was a convert.

His chest rose and shuddered unevenly as he took a big gasping sigh and let it out, his breathing settling right down.

She grinned. Lifted herself up on her elbow so she could look down at him, and said, "Now that you've recovered, ready to go again?"

HIS GAZE WIDENED in shock, a startled laugh escaping.

He cuddled her close. "Anytime, any place," he said.

She snickered and relaxed down beside him.

He was so damn grateful for this moment, he just wanted to squeeze her harder. She'd been...well, he was speechless. In trying to make it good for her, trying to make it special, and he'd been so surprised at the depth of his own need, his own response, hell, it had ended up...perfect.

"Thank you." That gentle voice floated up from within his arms. He had to question that he'd really heard them. He twisted slightly so that he could see her face and the look on her eyes.

"For what?" he murmured. Now what was she worrying about inside that pretty head of hers?

"For making it good for me."

Leaning over her, Weaver stared down at her in astonishment. "My pleasure," he whispered, dropping a kiss on the corner of her mouth. "This isn't a one-person activity. Both should be just as involved."

She gave a tiny shrug, but the matching smile on her lips caught his eye. "That might be true, but we also know it's not always that way. I'm not sure I could have had that same experience with another man."

He pulled back slightly. "Hell, I don't want to think of

you with another man," he said, "But I can't allow you to think that. There are many men in the world, and many are very experienced and good lovers," he admitted. "With way more experience than I—"

"Experience has nothing to do with it," she whispered. "It has to do with caring. With wanting me to be happy. To find pleasure. You helped me reach through a very difficult thing. The first time for any woman can be traumatizing. In my case, it was a mix of issues. Thank you for being you. I managed to trust you enough to do this and..." That beautiful smile of hers deepened. "And you gave me so much more than I expected."

Her words were lovely, the tone perfect. The sincerity...well, he'd never been thanked for doing something he'd wanted to do so badly. But he remembered that there'd been no pain. No hymen to break. He wondered about mentioning it then decided it wasn't the time. Later, when she was more comfortable, then maybe she'd share. Right now he was just so damn glad to be where he was. He wanted her to come back to this point in time and remember it with joy, not heartache.

She looked so lovely in his arms, such a perfect fit, his heart swelled. He gave her a tiny grin. "Yeah? Well in that case, let's see what we can do for round two."

And he lowered his head, gratified to find her lips already reaching up for him.

This woman was all about giving.

He'd never met anyone quite like her.

Then he couldn't think as her hand slid down his back to his buttocks and squeezed. Her toes slowly climbed his calves, and he realized she hadn't just enjoyed the first time around. She had learned. As she slid her hand between them to find him, his eyes crossed.

"Christ," he whispered as her fingers closed around him, her body sliding lower and lower.

She'd learned a hell of a lot.

CHAPTER 27

THE NEXT MORNING Paris woke slowly, confused by the aches and pains mixed with the delicious sensations throughout her body. She lay quiet for a long moment until the memories of last night filtered into place. Weaver. She smirked. A beautiful name. He'd woven a beautiful experience together for her. A night to never forget. A memory to cherish forever.

Hoping they had many more to come, she smiled at the thought of them as a pair.

She rolled over to find his side of the bed empty, the bedding thrown back as if in a hurry. She sat up, pushing her tousled hair back and looking around. She caught sight of her reflection in the massive television screen. Even in there, she looked well loved.

For the first time, she realized that's exactly what she was. Loved.

She hopped out of bed to look for a note or something to explain where Weaver had gone. Nothing. Hating the building worry that he'd walked away, she stepped into a hot shower and soaped herself all over. She'd have loved to have Weaver in there with her right now. Maybe later tonight. It was her last night here.

That reminder slowed her strokes as she used the washcloth on her skin. Her face. She had some decisions to make.

They weren't something she could make so easily.

But time was running out.

Back in her room, she realized there was still no sign of Weaver. It was almost time for the seminar. She'd forgotten to check the time before going into the shower and now she was late.

She quickly dressed, then raced down to the restaurant, grabbed two coffees, and hurried toward the conference room. There was a group of law enforcement off to one side. She skirted around them, keeping her head down and going around the centerpiece in the lobby. When she figured it was safe, she went to turn back and heard a voice that made her smile. Weaver.

Glancing in his direction, she almost dropped her coffee. He was speaking with Delaney. She froze, trying to assimilate what she was seeing. And couldn't find any reason that made her feel good. She turned and ran into the seminar room. Shit. Standing in the middle of the room she didn't know what to do. With stricken eyes, she searched the place she normally sat to find two coffees sitting there, waiting. She proceeded slowly, her heart desperate for an explanation but her mind coming up blank.

Weaver knew how devastating that man's presence was to her.

Was he trying to do something for her? Against her? A small shudder went down her long frame. She sat down before her legs gave out, but…

"Hey, are you all right? You look like you've had a horrible shock," a man sitting in front of her asked.

She tried for a smile. "I did actually. But I'm okay."

Busying herself with trying to organize all the cups on the table, she tried to reorganize the thoughts in her mind.

All she could see was the word *betrayal* flashing in neon colors in her mind.

Again.

WEAVER, ANGRY AND disturbed, slipped into class. He saw Paris already in her seat, and his smile bloomed fully when he saw the double set of cups on the table. He loved that about her. She rarely thought about herself and was always looking about to help others. He imagined nursing to be one of the best professions for her.

"Hey," he murmured to her bent head as he sat down.

He'd expected a wide grin, even a shy blush.

But she kept her head down and said, "Hey back."

He stared at her bent head in dismay. Damn. He hadn't wanted to leave her in bed this morning. He'd planned to wake her up in a special way, but he'd gotten a call from Jenna. Against his better judgment, he'd left the bedroom. And left her.

Alone.

He tried to see her face, but she had her head down enough that her hair fell to cover her features. Reaching across, he squeezed her shoulders and tried to make contact. She stiffened but didn't look at him.

Shit. He eased his hand back and turned to snag up one of the coffees. Hating that he felt like he was in the wrong, he took a drink and tried to pay attention. Jenna was setting up for a special set of exercises. The dynamic way she held the audience was inspiring. The way they all paid attention, as if she had the answers to life in the palm of her hand. Maybe she did.

It would be nice if she could share some of that smoothness. Especially with Paris. But circumstances kept him separated from her all morning and although he tried to catch a glimpse of her, she never looked his way. Was she regretting their night together?

With his heart sinking, he wondered how badly he'd screwed up. Then he got mad because if leaving her this morning was a deal breaker, then she should have let him know ahead of time.

Then again, she'd never been in this situation. She might not have any idea how etiquette worked.

Or maybe she was regretting last night.

Wouldn't that be his luck, the best night in his life and she wanted nothing more to do with him? Damn it. If that happened, life *was* a bitch.

Just then he was forced to put his focus elsewhere as his group ended up being the first to take on Jenna's exercises and for the next few hours, he didn't have time to think about last night or Paris's odd behavior. In fact, there wasn't much time to do anything. When they finally did break for lunch, he turned to find her and instead realized she was leaving with her group. Uncertainly, he watched her leave the hotel with them, willing her to look back and check on him.

She kept on walking.

"Come on, Weaver. You're coming for lunch with us. There's a lovely Japanese restaurant around the corner."

Japanese food was the last thing he wanted, but they wouldn't accept his excuses. And maybe he was better off not alone. Confused and angry now, he couldn't imagine what would happen if he let himself travel further down that path.

What the hell had he done?

CHAPTER 28

IT WAS HARD to reconcile the Weaver she'd known intimately last night with the man listening to Constable Delaney this morning. Her euphoria over the wonderful loving she'd received had turned to dust in her mouth. She didn't have a clue what to say to him now. She wished it was Friday and the workshop was over so she could leave. But it wasn't. She had one more night. This morning she'd have done anything to have that last night with him.

Now she couldn't get away fast enough. Although sitting at a restaurant with a group that didn't include him was the best she could do at the moment.

At the same time, a part of her said that wasn't fair. Until she talked to him, she couldn't know for sure that he'd betrayed her.

Since she'd trusted him last night, she wanted to trust him today.

If she hadn't seen the two men talking, then her day would be so different. Now she could barely look at him and when she did, it was to assess him. Study him. To look for that strip of character that said her trust wasn't misplaced.

Of course, she was well on her way to loving this man. To caring for him in a way she'd never cared for anyone before. And it terrified her and confused her, because it was all so new.

And if she was wrong in her interpretation of what she'd seen – then he had every right to be seriously angry with her. Tired of the mental ramble in her head, she rubbed her sore temple, wishing she could escape to her room. But it wasn't to be. She had said she'd come for lunch and looking around the Japanese restaurant, she realized the change would be good for her. She loved group lunches at work. They were fun and interactive. Not personal.

Right now, that's just what she needed.

The door blew open, letting another group into the restaurant. And damn if it wasn't Weaver's group. With a sense of inevitability, she watched Weaver walk in. He stood there, tall, cool, composed – personally she preferred the man who'd come apart in her arms – but there was no doubt this man had a presence. Her mind flashed to the previous night, their bodies in sync with one another.

Then his gaze caught hers. Locked and held hers captive. He strode toward her.

Frowning at him, she debated fleeing.

She hated public arguments. He'd better not start anything right now.

Her mouth opened to say something first, only he reached her, scooped her up, and sealed the words bubbling out of her mouth with a hot, rousing kiss.

She sagged against him, and her anger melted away as she dimly heard the cheers rolling through the restaurant all around them. He released her and with his breath warm against her ears, he whispered. "I don't know what the problem is, but this distance between us is over. I'd never…do anything to hurt you."

Calmly, he sat her back down on her chair. Then he snagged an empty chair from another table and created a space for himself right beside her.

WHEN SHE MELTED in his arms, he'd known he made the right decision. It had been a spontaneous decision. He hated to think he was as primitive as his ancestors, but it had felt like staking a claim. Her response had made the agreement public.

God, he'd loved how quickly her shock had turned to enthusiasm and straight into complete surrender. It was that honesty he needed in his life. To know he could trust that response. People often lied with their words, but their bodies showed the truth.

And he loved her truth.

He'd stunned her and likely the whole workshop group, but everyone loved a happy ending, and damn, he was determined that would be their story. Sure, they had issues. The workshop and the cop for two of them, but after tomorrow, both would be over. Both impediments to their future gone. He just had to hang in there until…

He was sure they could do that.

He looked down at her and realized she appeared very distracted, out of it. Leaning back, staring down at their entwined fingers, his protective instincts rose to the surface. Dropping a gentle kiss on her forehead, when the waitress came around the table to his side, he quickly ordered for them both. He knew she had to be hungry. Whatever had been churning inside had to be eating at her. Time for her to fill up and give all the stress something else to work on.

She was an amazing person and she'd been doing so well.

He wanted to do anything he could to help her.

A thought struck him. He'd been so focused on helping

Paris, he'd forgotten about his own needs. Then he stopped. No.

Originally he *had* been looking at his next professional step. While he hadn't thought to be lucky enough to find a partner anytime soon, when he'd turned around – there she was.

Now all he had to do was keep her there.

Paris was his. No ifs, ands, or buts. She just had to wake up and see the same thing he saw – they were meant for each other.

Seriously satisfied, he tucked her more comfortably against him and turned his attention to the others.

CHAPTER 29

H ER HEAD STILL singing, her heart still stuttering in her
shock, her body hummed with joy and expectation
over what was hopefully going to happen next…. Paris just
sat, tucked up against Weaver's side, his arm wrapped
around her shoulders, as the bubbly conversation flowed
around them.

The duality of the situation presented itself as she wanted to stay there like a limp attachment and never let go, yet
she also wanted to smack him. Then ask him what the hell
he'd been doing talking to *that* cop.

And she realized that's where she'd gone wrong; judging
him and walking away, not letting him back into her space
until he'd *taken* his spot back. She'd never asked him about
what she'd seen.

Never given him a chance to explain. So scared and panicked, she'd just sort of locked down inside until he'd taken
matters into his own hands. It never occurred to her that any
man would care for her enough to do that.

Thank heavens. She nestled into him, relishing his familiar smell and warmth.

The lunch arrived with a more than normal set of confusion with the double tables now combined and people no
longer in their original seats. As a plate was set down in front
of her, she started in surprise. She actually didn't remember

ordering.

"Hope this is okay," Weaver said. "I ordered for both of us."

How very controlling of him. No. She stopped and took a deep breath. How very caring. She was obviously still out of everything mentally, and he'd done what he could to smooth over any awkward moments. That was something she loved about him.

And then it hit her. Oh Lord. What if he'd been telling the cop to leave her alone?

Pulling back, she stared at him in stricken silence. Had she made such a big mistake against someone who'd only shown her kindness?

His gaze darkened as he caught her glance. Opening her mouth to say something, she suddenly became aware of their huge audience. She closed her mouth and pleaded for forgiveness with her eyes.

He opened his arm and tugged her back up close. Against her hair, he whispered, "Whatever it is that's wrong, we'll fix it. It's okay."

A shudder rippled down her back, an uncontrollable reaction to knowing she hadn't blown something so special.

"Did you hear me?"

She nodded, but the movement was stifled by the fact she was wedged up against his chest.

"Good. Then let's eat and keep the attention we're at-tracting to a minimum."

Right. She was making a spectacle of herself. She took a deep breath and straightened, then turned to face the others watching her curiously. She glanced down at her heaping plate then over at everyone else's normal side plate and said,

"Let me guess, Weaver ordered for me."

Laughter broke out across the table.

"Hey, I know this girl," Weaver said. "And boy, can she eat."

Feeling blessed and once again back to normal, Paris picked up the first bite of the California roll and popped it into her mouth. Her world was good.

WELL, THANK HEAVENS for that. He'd been trying to figure out how to get back into her good graces, and it looked like he'd managed it.

For the moment.

For Paris, he'd do a lot to keep the peace. Relationships were filled with ups and downs, but they needed a foundation to be able to weather the changing tide. A couple of days in a workshop and one night of hot sex was not a foundation. It was, however, a starting point, and he'd take it. Last night had been an eye-opener for him. About himself and about her. The freedom she'd shown, the lack of restraint – she'd been wild – for her own joy and for his.

He'd never made love before.

That's what was different. At least he thought so. It would take some more thinking about. He'd had sex before. Had been in several relationships, but he wasn't sure that depth of emotion had ever been there. He'd been good friends with his wife, but the relationship had been comfortable, not passionate. The memories of last night swirled through him, making it hard to keep his mind on the lunch before him. Keeping her left hand in his right hand while they ate left him only his left hand to eat with. Something he wasn't being very good at. But he'd rather look awkward and ridiculous than lose that physical contact.

"Here, try this." As he turned to face her, he saw a sample of something coming toward him. She laughed, her beautiful eyes twinkling as she popped the morsel into his mouth.

"It looked like you were starving."

His lips quirked and he squeezed her hand. "In that case, feel free to feed me."

"Ha, that would mean sharing, and you know how great I am at that."

He snorted. "You're just plowing through your lunch and hoping to be done fast so you can polish off my plate," he joked, loving the camaraderie. He caught several looks from the other attendees and a few were curious, but more were envious. And he realized how special this week had been. It wasn't over, but it was damn close. Things were winding down. Tonight was the one-on-one for him with Jenna and likely for Paris as she hadn't had one yet. Then tomorrow were projects followed by other speakers and wind-up sessions. Jenna always concluded on a Friday so the participants had the weekend to recuperate at home before they had to rejoin the real world. Smart strategy.

After today, he was feeling on the worn-out side himself. The emotional roller coaster had been brutal and he wasn't off yet. Might not get onto a stable platform for a long time.

And he wouldn't want it any other way. Not if Paris was that platform. He needed her. Her joy. Her insecurity. Her hope.

As he got to know her more, he realized in many ways she had done a better job of recuperating than he had.

She could show him a thing or two.

And after last night, he was dying to show her a few

more things. He grinned and gave up on utensils with his left hand. He used his fingers and started to make a decent inroad into the various rice rolls on his plate.

CHAPTER 30

PARIS FINISHED HER plate, happy and content. She watched, a smirk on her face, as Weaver gave up on decorum and let hunger rule. No one said anything as he used his fingers. It was working for him, so she didn't have a problem keeping his hand clasped in hers.

In fact, she wasn't sure she could let him go. It was that nice. That important to keep that connection there. She needed it, and she needed him. They fit together in a way she had never anticipated being possible.

In her heart she knew he was right, they could work this out.

As he finished lunch, she got a text from Jenna confirming the time for her evening session. She responded, giving her an affirmative. It was going to be at seven-thirty tonight. A bit late, but doable. Jenna's schedule was brutal, she knew. And she was lucky to have made as much progress as she had before her session with Jenna. It wouldn't have made sense to have her session early in the week. She'd still be floundering.

Though she still was in many ways, she had come further than she'd expected thanks to Weaver. It was shocking how his gentle persistence had won her over.

When was his session with Jenna? Maybe it would be around the same time so they could be together afterwards.

The group finished their meals, paid their bills in a mess

of laughter and confusion, and stood up. She let go of his hand and murmured something about going to the ladies' room.

In the small room she stared at her face, seeing the fatigue from the night with little sleep and the hated confused emotions that had been rolling through her all morning. Using the facilities, she washed up, taking a moment to slap cold water on her cheeks and burning eyes. She still had the afternoon to get through.

Somehow, knowing she had Weaver at her side again, she knew she'd make it.

A text came in as she was walking back to the front door. Sean.

She smiled and read the simple question asking how she was doing.

He was a special brother. She responded, telling him she was much better and now looking forward to getting through the rest of the workshop.

His instant response took some of the joy out of the communication.

Did you talk to Delaney?

It was her first reaction not to answer, but she knew he would not leave it alone. She gave him a short answer. *No.* Then in a separate text she added, *I can't.*

Though he might be disappointed, he wouldn't judge her. She hated disappointing him though. As far as she'd come in life, he'd been there rooting for her the whole time. Knowing more than anyone what she had been through, he wanted her to see this guy. Deal with it and move on. Just the thought was setting the bile in her gut seething. Talk about a big issue.

Her footsteps slowed as she walked through the restaurant. After all she had learned this week, she wanted to be big enough to handle this. She needed to be. Maybe she could set a date down the road, like in six months' time. Time to prepare for the meeting. Time to adjust.

Time to panic and find ways of getting out of it.

She sighed. Confused and depressed suddenly by her own lack of resolve, she opened the front door and walked into the sunshine. Outside, she joined the group and found Weaver waiting for her.

He searched her face. "Tired?"

She nodded and turned to fall into step behind the other attendees heading back to the hotel. "A little."

"Looks more like life is hitting you a little sideways."

"True enough." But she wasn't ready to share her problem and the gut-wrenching decision she needed to make. So much in her life had been hard. How hard could this one be? Or maybe a better question was if she were to look back on her life in a year, would she be happy? She'd been strong enough to make this step and ashamed she'd been so weak. Once again incapable of doing what she needed to do. A failure.

Just that word made her cringe.

Instead of sharing, she said, "What's it going to take to have you move past needing Justice for your father?"

He stared at her, as if he hadn't been expecting the change in topic. There was silence for a long time. She winced. "Sorry, I shouldn't have brought it up."

"You're entitled. We're doing a lot of pushing boundaries just because we're here but also because we're involved," he said calmly. "But you made me realize something I hadn't considered before." Their eyes locked and their hands clasped together. "It's not that I'm not willing to share, I'm just not sure where all this revelation leaves me in this situation."

"Oh, well maybe that's a good thing then." She smiled. "It would be nice to see you grow through this workshop too."

"I'm growing more than I thought possible," he admitted with a smile. "Maybe that's why I'm stuck for an answer. It seems to me my instinctive response has changed and I need to think about it."

"Good enough," she said lightly. "When you figure it out, will you let me know?"

HE SQUEEZED HER hand. "Sure. It's an important issue for you, isn't it?"

She gave him a serious nod. "It is."

Interesting. Curious, but also a little confused, he stayed quiet trying to work through it. He knew Justice was a big one for her. It was for him too. But maybe not as big as it had been in the past.

And why was that?

He'd held that up as a flag in front of him for a long time. It had been very important. As if he could solve that and that would give him peace over the issue. Make peace with his past. Make peace with his childhood. Have someone to blame. The killer. If he'd not taken his father away, then Weaver's childhood wouldn't have been so horrible. So if he had someone to blame, then he wouldn't have to take on any of the responsibility himself. Then why should he? He'd been a child and he'd done what he could to survive.

And he'd done that part quite well. Sure, there'd been a lot of hiccups. But in many ways, it had been smooth sailing forward. So why was he hanging on to that issue as if to say it still made a difference? Yes, he'd like to see his father's killer caught and pay the price. Was it likely to happen? Maybe and maybe not. Did he want to hang onto all that emotion and energy that was pulling him down?

But it wasn't pulling him down. He didn't feel like there was any weight there. No emotional tug as he considered the missing man in his life. Not anymore.

Why?

As he walked, it became clear that he'd already let it go. Somewhere in the last few years, he'd come to realize that his father had died young and it was a horrible shame for all involved. Including his mother. She'd been unable to move on, and he'd taken her methodology as his own and held up his father's death as a major roadblock in his life. Except, in the intervening years, he'd formed his own methods of dealing with his life. Ones that suited him.

Not hers that kept her locked up in a crumpled-up space of time and emotion.

But ones that freed him from those bonds.

A child learned from his or her parents. That was the way of the world. He knew that. He'd been taught that, he'd seen it over and over again and knew it well. But at one point in time, a child also had to determine when and how he wanted to relate to the world around him as an individual. Either he further developed the tools his parents gave him or he learned his own coping skills.

If the latter, at one point the original coping skills became redundant and fell away from disuse.

Just like his had.

After a while, he'd learned to look at life differently. All the patients he'd seen and interacted with through grad school and had been blessed to have been a part of their process had taught him something even if it had taken him until now to understand. Maybe nothing major in the sense of an aha moment, but they'd slowly built up to show him what he wanted for himself and what he didn't want for himself.

His own wife had done the same thing. But he hadn't seen it. It had been her intense purpose to get married as she'd needed that security. That foundation. She hadn't been able to go forward with their relationship until that happened. Being ambivalent about the legal side of marriage, he'd agreed.

When after six months, she'd turned and said, "Thank you, I can move past this stage now," he'd been literally stunned.

And angry. Very angry. He'd been happy married to her. Thought she'd been happy. And she had, until she realized that it wasn't marriage she was looking for as much as having *been* married. So she had caught up to where everyone else in her world was at for her age level. She'd been so afraid that marriage would slip past her, be an old maid so to speak, and she'd been sure that being married would make her happy.

Only to realize she not only didn't want to be married but didn't really want to be with him at all.

After he'd gotten over the hurt and anger, he realized she'd also been a good lesson for him. She'd done what she needed to do and moved on. Regardless of whom she hurt.

For him, he had not moved on because he hadn't wanted to hurt or be hurt. His wife had tramped around in his life for a good year and by the time it was over, he could see she was doing much better having understood where her own issues had been at.

As she had explained to him, "You're part of my past now. And I'm ready to leave all that garbage behind."

Not nice.

To find he'd been part of the 'garbage' hurt. But it wasn't the same thing as to find his love unrequited. Because he hadn't really loved her in the first place. There was an attraction for sure and he'd cared for her a lot. More, he'd been content. Hadn't cared to get married as he'd seen no need. That meant a further commitment that wasn't required – wasn't wanted, he realized now.

His fault. He hadn't looked at his motives. Or hers. They hadn't discussed why the marriage. They hadn't really done anything but take the step she felt she needed to "feel secure." That she didn't miss out on something she thought was important until she was married.

Now he understood it. Even though it had been painful, he learned to look at relationships differently. He'd been avoiding anyone in therapy so to avoid a second scenario like his wife.

And he hadn't come to the workshop to do anything other than take notes for his paper.

And while he hadn't been looking, Paris had shown up.

And blown him away.

Therapy might not be done for her and she might need help again in the future, but her self-awareness was amazing. It was clear to her why she should do something and why she couldn't do something.

He couldn't argue with that.

She was doing the best she could.

CHAPTER 31

T HE AFTERNOON WAS traumatic. Paris watched one woman break down completely and require help to leave the room. She felt close to tears many times as they dealt with the term *dreams*. Dreams they held and dreams they felt they could never have.

And how to modify those dreams to be something they could have.

By the time Jenna called the end of the day, there was a film of sweat over Paris's skin and her eyes burned with unshed tears. The emotional workout had been harder than anything she'd expected to have. Just the thought of packing up her stuff and making her way to her room made her want to just roll over and die.

Weaver stepped in front of her.

Gazing up at him, she was not ready or willing to stand up. And realized he looked about the same. She held out a hand and he clasped it, helping her up. "I think the rooms are too far away," she murmured.

He nodded. "Today they are."

But his voice was gritty, strained.

"Hard afternoon for you too, huh?"

Wide-eyed and serious, his head drooped, and damn if there wasn't a brightness to his eyes she'd not seen before. She squeezed his hand in commiseration and grabbed her purse. "I'm ready."

After leading her out into the lobby, he stopped and said, "Which way?"

"Outside," she said suddenly. "Fresh air and flowers. Sunshine and new growth."

Gaze brightening, he nodded. Together they walked out into the sunshine, the hustle and bustle of the busy city streets. The sheer normality of their surroundings.

Not talking, they walked, automatically heading to the water and the boats they'd seen earlier. It was a ten-minute walk, but its curative effects were wonderful. She could feel the constriction around her chest easing and the bands knotting her stomach breaking up. By the time they found a bench to sit on and watch the world on the water, she could breathe normally.

"How does she do that?" she asked in a low voice. "This is the last full day and there were so many things happening, so many people breaking down. Stuff coming up for everyone. I've never been through anything so intense."

"And that's still going to continue. Tonight, overnight, and all day tomorrow. I don't know if they are all like this but with this level of intensity, it's no wonder her workshops get such wonderful results."

"It's not what I expected when I started a few days ago," she murmured. She wasn't even sure what had happened today. Lots of father stuff. Stuff about value. Having value. Deserving to be valued. Lots of emotional letting go of the bonds she'd carried for so long. "The stuff we do and did, the stuff we believed, a lot of it is so stupid."

"Only now that you can look back and see what it's like as an adult," Weaver said. "As a child, a teen, it's impossible. We absorb the environment around us. We learn from those abusing us. We grow based on everything – one direction or another."

Quietly contemplative, Paris sat for a moment then said, "Do you know my father told me I was the reason my mother left? And I believed him? Didn't think I was worthy of love. Didn't think I could be a mother because my mother had walked out on us, so what if I did the same? Figured that if I had been a 'good girl,' my father would forgive me for forcing her to leave and he'd love me too."

Weaver growled by her side. "That's what I mean. A child just wants to be loved, and they are so open to all influences. It's amazing that any of us can make it through childhood with our sanity intact."

That made her smile. "Maybe that's why so many of us are screwed up."

"You're not screwed up," he said instantly. "You're busy trying to unscrew all the twists and turns and emotional blackmail your father put you through. Not your fault."

"No, maybe not, but I still don't feel quite normal."

"There is no normal for anyone. That's a myth." He smiled down at her. "The trick is to find a *normal* that suits you."

She liked the sound of that. "You'd make a great psychologist. I'm glad you've gone in that direction."

"Ha." The sound he made had a little humor behind it, but was sadder. She turned to look at him. "I mean it. You're a great listener and you understand how all this works. You will be great."

He didn't look convinced. "I don't think I'm ready. I still have so much of my own crap to deal with. And I am affected by the growth of those around me."

Her gaze widened. "Why are either of those impediments?"

"They just are." He shrugged.

"No, that's your insecurity talking. Sure, you might not be ready to do this full-time today, or tomorrow even. Maybe you need to go back to school or do a practicum." She threw an arm out wide. "I don't know how this works, but it seems to me you'd be a natural. I think that's why Jenna was willing to help you with your paper. She saw the potential in you as well."

He studied her closely, as if wondering if her words had merit. "I doubt it, but thanks. And there isn't going to be a paper on the workshop. I couldn't do it. I became too attached to what was happening."

"What? But that was important to you."

"Jenna seemed to think publications would help me, so maybe she's willing to consider a different topic."

"But I thought that's why you came here this week."

"It was, but it's not why I stayed." He twisted on the bench seat until he could look at her. "I stayed because of you."

"I like the sound of that." She smiled at him. "And I'm glad you stayed, but I wish you'd been able to do the paper too."

"I needed something else from this week, and that was of more value."

"Maybe, but it seems like a waste to miss out on publishing credits."

He shrugged. "Maybe, but right now my mind is overwhelmed, and when I'm learning and growing as much as I am, it's hard to be detached."

"So leave it a week and write up something. It will be more personal. It will be your own story and referenced to those of us who were here – without names or personal information – but still valid."

The rhythmic lapping of the water drew her gaze, then he said, "We'll see. Today isn't over yet. And could still be difficult."

"I know. I have my session with Jenna tonight."

"So do I."

"What time?"

"Six-thirty."

"Oh, I'm at seven-thirty. I'd rather be earlier," she said, staring out across the water. It was glassy and calm with nary a breeze. So different from the last time she watched the boats fight against the waves. Now in contrast, sailboats lulled in the ocean, not moving, just sitting there.

She wondered at their sluggish movements. They must have motors onboard to be able to get home in weather like this. Otherwise they were stuck.

Kinda like she'd been on the first day of the course. Weaver had been her engine. He'd gotten her moving in all kinds of directions.

"We could switch if you want. Just show up with me at my time and we'll ask her." There was an odd tone in his voice. She stared at him, but he was staring moodily across the water at the same floating sailboat she had been watching earlier.

"Sure, that sounds good." And it did. She wanted it over with so she could go to her room and know this tough day was over. Being peeled from the inside out was brutal.

It hurt to have an open, constantly oozing type of wound. Then you actually gave permission for someone like Jenna to go in there and scrape out a little more. Talk about pain.

"So, food first then?" she asked, wondering if she was even hungry. If she really wanted to be bothered. She was just so tired. And with more to come, she knew the tears would flow. Her stomach always ached then.

"Afterward," he said. "That afternoon ran really late today. It's already six o'clock. We've been sitting here like zombies for forty minutes already."

"Zombies – good term." And it made sense to eat afterward. She was a little worried about him though. There was something else bothering him and he seemed really depressed. She reached out and held his hand. "Thanks for being there today."

It crossed her mind to bring up Delaney, but at the same time she didn't. Why ruin the moment? And they were both so tired that if things got out of hand, they'd say things they would both regret. Not a good scenario. Get through tonight. Then tomorrow was the project. A project they hadn't done. She hadn't even done today's homework. She was pretty sure Weaver was in the same boat. They'd been a little too preoccupied last night to even consider homework. Now the project faced them. And she had no idea what to do about that. She kept hoping for a miracle. Some insight that would give them a quick and easy answer.

The sailboat was still wallowing on the horizon. Like she'd been doing. And like her, until that wind came along, it wasn't going anywhere.

She sighed.

Turning her into him for a hug, he asked, "You okay?"

She nodded. "I will be. I just want tonight over with."

"Me too. Let's head back. I could use another coffee."

She laughed. "We drink too much of that stuff."

"True, but it keeps me going. Especially now."

Slowly, as neither had the energy to move quickly, they made their way back to the hotel. At the restaurant, she took a look at the food behind the counter and realized she'd had enough muffins for the day. Likely for the week. They took their coffees and meandered through the hotel until they came to the small room Jenna had been using for her one-on-one sessions.

They were early. The room was empty.

"I'm so tired I just want to sleep," she said, collapsing into a chair.

"Understandable." There was a pause then he said, "Given last night and everything else going on around here, it's amazing you are still functioning."

"True enough," she said, wondering about the sensibility of her upcoming session. "I wonder if I should try to cancel Jenna's session."

He looked at her in surprise. "Why would you do that?"

"Because I'm so tired. Because my defenses are down. Because she's likely to see way more than I want her to see."

"Isn't that a good thing?"

A laugh burbled out. "Maybe, but I still have to be strong enough to deal with the aftermath."

"True." He gave a sad sigh. "Oh so true. And tonight being the last night, it's likely to be harder than ever."

"Exactly."

There was a commotion at the door. She turned, noticing that Weaver stared straight ahead, a grim look on his face.

And watched Jenna walk in.

With Constable Delaney.

She gasped in shock and turned to face Weaver, pleading for help. But he closed his eyes and slumped into his chair.

Shit.

He already knew.

She'd been ambushed.

Betrayed.

HE WASN'T READY for this. Finally, he had found something precious and he was going to lose it. Why him? Why couldn't they have done this without him? He'd only agreed to bring her here. If she wanted to walk, they had to let her walk. Was she ready? He doubted it. But he was going to be there for her regardless. If she'd let him.

He figured she'd turn, slap him, and walk away.

And he'd lose her.

Why would she trust him after this?

He stood up and faced the other two. He nodded a greeting.

"She gets to leave if she wants to," he said in a hard voice. Yet contradicting his own words, he held Paris's hand in a tight grip. She tried to tug her hand free. He wouldn't let her. Her touch was essential. He needed the contact, even if she was unwilling. He heard her gasp and felt her shock but didn't dare look at her. Desperately, he willed her to have the strength to do this. And yet if she couldn't, he wanted her to have the opportunity to walk out.

Jenna walked forward, a lovely smile on her beautiful face. "Hi, Paris."

Paris shook her head and shuffled backward a half step. Weaver felt the movement.

He looked down at her, seeing the shakes already racking her body, and said, "This has to be her choice."

CHAPTER 32

JENNA SAID IN a quiet voice, "Sometimes there is more than one person who needs healing in a certain situation."

Paris froze. Weaver's hand gripped hers securely. She didn't think she could run if she tried. Had he set her up? He'd had some part in it. Is that why he'd looked so defeated? So tired?

She didn't want to be here. She didn't want to face him. Hell, she didn't want to face any of them.

But as Jenna talked, Paris realized that although the panic was at her throat and her breath refused to cooperate, her hand was gripping Weaver's as hard as his was gripping hers. She was holding on to him. Her rock.

But what if he had set her up?

It *should* matter.

Then Jenna's words hit home. Slowly, she raised her head to stare at her. She knew she looked confused and terrified. There was no way she didn't, but Jenna, outside of the very gentleness in her voice, didn't seem to care.

"And sometimes, crossing that barrier can be the hardest thing we've ever done," Jenna said. "For both parties."

Paris shook her head. What was she talking about? There weren't two parties involved. There was just her...

She dared not look at the constable.

"Constable Delaney needs to talk to you. You need to talk to him. I'm here to facilitate that conversation if both parties are willing to let it happen. I'm not here to force it. This has to be your choice."

Tears welled up in Paris's eyes. How was any of this a choice?

"Just remember," Jenna said. "You are loved, and people want to see you through this. No matter how hard it can be."

"Hard," Paris cried. "Do you know *how* hard this is?" She still refused to look at the constable.

"No, I don't. And I can't until you tell me." Jenna was so comfortable, so calm, coming from such a heart position, it was damn hard to get mad at her for being the guardian angel of their souls whether Paris liked it or not.

"I'm sorry." That muttered, almost gruff voice came from the doorway, slightly behind Jenna. A voice from her past.

Sorry? She was so confused. Why was he sorry? Why was he even here? He was stalking her. Surely he should be in trouble for that. But no, the cops got away with murder. At that thought, her shoulders slumped and she collapsed to the chair, her hand still clutching Weaver's. No, she'd been the one to get away with murder.

The voice continued. "Years ago when I met you, I'd just joined the team and was actually brand new to your case. The rest of the team would have been better off talking to you. I know that now. Back then, I didn't. I wasn't used to talking to traumatized teens. Hadn't expected to see what I saw."

Her shoulders and chest seemed to sink in on themselves and her eyes closed tightly as memories pulled her back in time. A time when life hadn't held rainbows or unicorns.

There'd only been pain and darkness.

"I said some things I shouldn't have."

He stopped for a moment, and then said. "In another circumstance the words might have been appropriate, but I read you wrong. I read the situation wrong." He took a deep breath and said, "For that, I'm sorry."

"What did you say?" Weaver asked in a hard voice.

The constable hesitated, then said, "I warned her not to do it again. That she'd liked it too much and it would become something she craved."

"It?"

"It's not my tale to tell," Delaney said. "I'd hoped to see that she'd become a wonderful adult and human being, that she'd moved past my words without a problem. But when I realized that she wouldn't see me, or acknowledge me, and worse, she ran from me – I knew my own fears had been correct."

For the first time, Paris turned to face him. The man who'd given her nightmares. The man who'd made her afraid of the one thing she'd never been afraid of before – herself.

"Paris?" Weaver asked in a hard voice. There was no arguing with that tone. He wanted to know what was going on, and he wanted to know now.

"I killed my father," she said.

She waited a beat, but there was only silence from Weaver. Silence from the other two. In a dull voice, she continued, "He beat me every day of my life. Sometimes for fun, sometimes because he was bored. Sometimes because he loved to hear me scream. And often to just punish my brother." She heard Weaver's subdued groan, but she was staring at the squiggly random pattern on the floor as her whole life had been a seemingly random pattern.

She dropped his hand and clenched her fists in her lap, the knuckles white. Weaver wouldn't want anything to do with her now. Knowing the truth, he'd know that she wasn't worthy. She didn't deserve him.

She lifted her gaze, her head was heavy with emotion, pain. "He was killing my brother, you know," she said in a calm, reasonable voice. "Daring me to do something about it. A favorite game of his. He'd beat one and yell at the other to fight him. Then he could turn and beat the second one down. Sean had been trying to save me when our father turned on him. He beat us often. Once so badly, he damaged my insides so I can't have children. In fact, surgery was required and I lost half my reproductive organs." She heard the shocked gasps from the others.

"But I'd have survived the physical damage, survived the emotional damage, except for one cop who warned me about liking it too much. That he saw how much I'd enjoyed the killing. That there was something inside of me that I needed to keep an eye on."

Delaney winced. Weaver moved forward, anger radiating from him.

"And you were right," she said calmly, her eyes shadowed with memories. "I did enjoy it. I did love knowing that he was taking his last breath while I stabbed him over and over again. I saved my brother – and likely myself."

She lifted her chin and stared defiantly at Delaney. "But you were the reason I lost sleep over and over again throughout the years. I enjoyed killing him because I'd been a beaten animal, desperate to live and to save the only other decent human being I knew in this world. I didn't enjoy the killing – I enjoyed killing *him*. Stopping him from hurting my brother. Hurting me. Over and over again. He never stopped. He was *never* going to stop."

Delaney nodded, an understanding on his face she hadn't expected to see. But the dam had been broken.

"All these years, I was afraid that I'd kill again. I went into nursing to try and help people. To absolve myself of the guilt of my actions. I love babies because I can never have them, thanks to that man who called himself my father. But more than that, a part of me was glad because it meant his evil genes couldn't be passed down through me. I was going to adopt, but that fear was always there in the back of my mind. What if I lost it and killed my own child? What if my father's evil lives in me – which it does – right?" she added in a hard mocking tone. "Because I've already killed once."

He opened his mouth to speak.

"And no," she said, steamrolling right over him. "I have no regrets – not really. I'd kill the bastard a dozen times over to save my brother. I never did it to save myself. I did it to save him."

Silence.

Then she added, "And I'd do it again." Her smile was glacier sharp, her eyes bright, hard. "And I'd enjoy it each and every time."

WEAVER STARED AT her, feeling his chest lock down and his gut slammed with pain. This was what was behind all her fears. She had killed her father.

He'd spent his lifetime looking for his father's murderer.

In stark contrast, she spent her lifetime looking at herself as her father's murderer.

Oh Jesus.

He couldn't imagine.

The room was silent. Paris stood up, tall and defiant, but he could see the thread of shivers continuously running through her. She was standing through guts alone. Then, that was Paris.

Waiting for a verdict, she stood silently. A judge and jury to take her away as she'd always suspected she deserved, or to be given a pass and would even then always wonder if she'd gotten off too lightly.

The defiance radiated from her, but not as an attitude. As a defense. She expected to be hauled out of here in handcuffs. All her life she really thought she'd done something wrong. That there was something wrong with her.

There wasn't. And to have spent a lifetime, first because of her father, then by her actions and the words of this cop – terrified of being defective – now that was criminal.

Glancing at Jenna's face, Weaver saw only compassion and maybe a hint of relief. He could relate. He was so proud of Paris.

A mixture of emotions crossed Delaney's face. Pain, regret, guilt.

Good.

The tableau had frozen and Paris's trembling increased. He knew she was heading for a complete breakdown. Calmly, steadily, he stepped to her side and hauled her up against his chest, his warmth slowing her shaking. In a voice loud enough for the rest to hear but especially so that there was no way she couldn't, he said. "And I'm glad you did."

Her back stiffened.

"Your father was a rabid animal out of control and had been for a long time. He was going to kill your brother and you eventually if you hadn't stopped him." Gently he massaged her hard, terrified muscles, hoping to find the right words to unlock a decade of fear and make it okay. "It's called self-defense for a reason."

Shaking her head, she tried twisting away from him. He grabbed her hand back. "Not the enjoyment. I'm sick. Inside. All I could ever think of was a life without him. A life where I didn't have to be afraid. A life of peace."

She broke off as her voice broke down. Then she pulled herself back slightly and regained control. "Other people kill in self-defense if they are attacked by a home invader or something similar. Not like I did."

"No," Jenna said, her tone oozing compassion, so gentle he thought surely it would bring Paris to tears. "They hadn't spent a lifetime being beaten by the one person who was supposed to care for them. They didn't spend hours and days watching those they loved getting beaten over and over again, and neither did they have the reason to do what you did. You know he wouldn't have stopped. You knew someone would have to kill him to make him stop."

"But why me?" she cried out brokenly. "It was the best thing to have happened yet I feel so guilty. Surely there was another way?" She turned slightly away.

"Maybe," Jenna said. "But most likely not. It would have been you or Sean. You know that because no one else was there. No one else was ever there. You two fought with this man every single day, but you didn't tell anyone, did you?"

When Paris shook her head, Jenna continued. "You did what you had to do to survive. You can say you did it to save Sean, and I believe you, but you also did it to save yourself. He'd have killed you next. Eventually he would have had to. He couldn't let you live to tell anyone what he'd done, could he?"

Paris gazed at her. Weaver stood by her side, his arm around her shoulders, holding her close. He'd be damned if she was going to think she was all alone here. She wasn't.

"I'm glad you had Sean all those years," he said gently. "You helped each other survive."

"I'd do anything for him," she whispered.

"You already did. You need to let that go."

She shook her head violently. "You can't just let something go. It's with me every single day. There isn't a day when I don't wonder if I'll ever do it again. If I might abuse a child of my own. If I might kill again."

"And that's normal and healthy," Jenna said. "We can't live with major events in our life without wondering about scenarios like that. Any more than you could sit there and wonder 'what if' you hadn't saved Sean that day? What if your mother hadn't run away? How different would your life be?"

At an odd sound beside her, she turned to Delaney.

"Barry? Do you have something to add to that point?"

He hesitated, then plunged in. "I had no idea your mother was missing. I thought she was deceased."

Paris stared at him. Weaver stared from her to him. "Do you know if she is?"

"No, I don't know, but I thought there was something in the files." He frowned. "I'm sorry. I'd have to look it up."

"She's missing," Paris said. "That's all I know. She walked away without warning."

"And who told you that?" Delaney asked.

"He did. He said she didn't want to be a mother anymore and she'd left. Pulled out in the middle of the night so she wouldn't have to face us and went back east."

The pain in her voice made Weaver want to snatch her back into his arms and take her away. But she needed to stand there and do this on her own for as long as she could.

"Did you have any communication afterwards?" Delaney asked, his voice calm, professional.

Weaver looked at him sharply then switched his gaze to Jenna. Did they know something?

Paris shook her head. "No, my birthday was the following week, and I'd hoped she'd contact me for that. She'd made plans for a small celebration, just the three of us, but then she ran," she said bitterly. "I never saw her again."

"What kind of celebration?" Jenna asked curiously.

"I don't really know. She said I couldn't mention it ever, but that we'd have a wonderful celebration, just the three of us."

There was a long silence.

"And did you see any of her stuff after she left?"

"I saw my father bagging up her clothes and personal belongings. He threw them into the truck and we hauled it away to the dump." Now tears glistened. "I wanted to keep a few things and he laughed at me. Told me she was gone and I'd never see her again. To throw all that shit away and forget about it. And her."

"He said that you'd never see her again?"

Paris nodded and wiped at the corner of her eyes. "Yes, he said it all the time as if to torment us. She'd hated us so much she couldn't stand the thought of being around us. I figure she found her chance to run and took it. For whatever reason, she couldn't take us or didn't want to take us with her."

And finally Weaver got it.

He winced. "You think her father killed her mother, don't you?"

CHAPTER 33

PARIS GASPED, HER gaze going from Weaver's to lock onto Delaney's face.

The constable shrugged. "I don't know for sure, but we certainly see that scenario over and over again in abuse situations. She might have been planning to leave with you – that might have been your birthday celebration – but he got wind of it. Tell me, were the beatings any worse afterwards?"

Paris found it hard to breathe. She remembered her mother as a gentle soul. She'd often fantasized that her mother had escaped the torture they'd all been through, but when there was never any contact, she'd lost that hope. Figured her mother had made a new life for herself. Maybe had more children.

And as the mind was wont to do, she'd considered her mother might have died, but she hadn't had any reason to believe it either way. It was easier to think she'd died in an accident and couldn't come back for them than to accept that she *wouldn't* come back.

"Is there any way to find out?" she asked. "With my father dead, we aren't likely to ever know for sure."

"Unless she's in our database as a Jane Doe."

Automatically, she nodded. There were too many shocks to know how to respond. She could only react. It hurt so much to consider her mother might be lying in a cold drawer or buried in an unmarked grave, unloved and unidentified.

"I'd like to do whatever I can to make sure she's not there."

"It's just a DNA test." He splayed out his hands. "The labs are all overworked, so there won't be any answers for a long time."

"I haven't had any answers up to now. If one day I get one, then that would bring closure."

"It might, but it's not the real issue here, Paris," Jenna spoke up. "The issue is you right now. You know your father needed to be stopped…"

"I know," Paris whispered, "But it's not easy to look at yourself and realize that you are capable of killing."

"We are all capable of killing," Jenna said, her voice a steady beacon in the storm. "And it's that much easier if you are trying to save loved ones. You aren't guilty of murder. You know that in the eyes of the law. But you are still afraid, aren't you."

Paris nodded. "What if they made a mistake?"

"They didn't," Delaney said. "The law was very clear in your case. You weren't let off the hook because you were *never* on the hook."

"And the things you said," she asked, getting more back-bone into her voice. She glared at the man whose words had tormented her since forever. "You believed them."

"I did at the time – at least, I worried that they might be true." He hesitated then plunged in. "I'd just come off a particularly difficult case where a young man had murdered his entire family, including an eighteen-month-old sister. In that case, he had enjoyed it. He'd enjoyed killing each and every one of them."

At her gasp, he nodded. "So when I saw you, having just

killed your own father, I was afraid it was a similar situation, just that side of you hadn't been developed as much as this other kid. I didn't want it to be true. I could see something in there, inside of you, but didn't know what I was seeing. I warned you to be careful and not let that feeling be something you chased. Because once you start killing for your highs in life, there's no way to stop."

She shook her head violently. "There was no high. I was sick for days. I couldn't keep food down and I couldn't stop shaking."

"Shock," Jenna said, "and to be expected. And before we gloss over this, it's important to understand that at that moment in time when you were saving Sean, you did enjoy it. You enjoyed finally being able to take control. Finally, you could do something about the pain and torment."

"I didn't enjoy it as much as I was so damn glad that I'd done it. That I'd picked up that knife and stopped him. I didn't think, honestly. I just reacted." Tears started pouring down her cheeks. "I kept telling him to stop, that he was killing him. He answered, 'Perfect. Good riddance to another one.'"

"Another?" asked Delaney. "Don't you see? In all likelihood, he killed your mother before you. You'd have been dead next."

She stared at him, hating the words, the concept, but realizing that he might be right. Relief bloomed ever so lightly inside. Like a tiny unfurling bit of hope. Maybe her mother hadn't abandoned her. "Maybe that's why she never came back for me."

Weaver squeezed her shoulder, making her aware for the first time that she'd spoken out loud. "She'd have come back if she could, you know that."

"I want to know that," she corrected. "But chances are, we'll never know for sure."

"I'd have to check out the files back then. See if a missing person's report was filed."

"He wouldn't have filed it," Paris said. "He wanted her gone. At least, he often made comments afterwards." Rubbing her pounding temple, she couldn't remember anything clearly anymore.

"I always knew she was gone for good." She was exhausted and worn out, but she realized what she'd always known inside. Her mother wasn't *ever* coming back. She couldn't. She was dead. Her childhood dreams of her mother escaping to a better life, maybe coming back to save her and Sean, were just that – dreams. Happier stories to help her get through the days.

"He killed her." She crumpled into a chair, her legs too weak to let her stand. "I think I always knew inside."

"Most likely he did. It would fit the pattern," Delaney said. "And given that, knowing he killed your mother, do you still think you did wrong? That you'd kill heedlessly in the future?"

Dazed, she stared at him, trying to assimilate what she knew now to her life, her thoughts, and her pain. Her future.

She shook her head. "Never." She held up a hand. "Unless someone was hurting those I love."

Weaver, the constable, and Jenna all spoke up at the same time and said the same word.

"Exactly."

Her gaze went from one to the other, hoping, searching, wanting to see the truth of their words.

And saw what she needed to see – her heart exploded with relief.

And she burst into tears.

WEAVER SNAGGED HER up and squeezed her tight. That she went into his arms so easily bruised his heart. She'd been through so much. Her and her brother. He closed his eyes and held her close, breathing deeply at all he had just learned. In the background, he could hear the cop speaking with Jenna. There was something about checking when the cop got back to the office. Weaver doubted that they'd find anything about Paris's mother after all this time. After all, look at his father's case. It was still open. However, she could now open a missing person's file on her mother and they'd learn what there was to learn. It was something.

If it wasn't enough, then he could help her deal with that.

That was a truth he'd been living for a long time.

If they did find out the truth, good or bad, he could help her deal with those issues too. In fact, he'd just like to be there to help her in whatever way he could. She'd helped him. He'd moved past many issues. Just from being around her, seeing her perspective.

And updating his own. That had been his problem — hanging onto the hurt. Paris had been badly hurt and had made it her goal to stuff it deep inside and go on in spite of it. In his case, he'd let the hurt stop him. He could have had relationships since his wife walked out. But he hadn't. It was easier not to. He had a tough childhood, but even his mother had been working on cleaning up her act.

He hadn't.

He didn't know if he believed it or not, but that was his past conditioning judging her. It was time to release that. Let it go and let her go. She was trying – that was all anyone could wish for.

Maybe he could check in on her. See if she wanted to see him. See if she wanted the connection. See if there was a connection to build on.

If not, nothing changed. But if there was, then like Paris said, he'd done without a mother for a long time.

Maybe it was time to change that.

CHAPTER 34

PARIS STOOD IN the circle of Weaver's arms. The stuffing was gone from her insides. If he hadn't been holding her up, she'd have slid to the floor a long time ago.

She didn't know where to go from here. Her history, her interpretation of events, the hurts, the pain, the sense of abandonment. Everything had changed. All of this information rolled around inside her head. Think about things – or maybe not think, just let sensations rise and fall. Let the lies fall away. The emotions rise and dissipate. Her life was changing from this point forward.

Thank heavens.

As if understanding, Weaver tightened his grip around her. Had he been a part of this? She figured he had. Was she upset about that? She had been earlier. Now... now she understood... maybe. Except her mind couldn't reconcile betrayal and helping. When did one become the other?

Then she heard voices in the background. Constable Delaney.

Should she let *him* off the hook? She understood now what he'd gone through. Where he'd been at in his life when he'd spoken to her. What his mental process had been coming in.

She'd been terrified back then. Had been looking for bogeymen in her world and with her father gone, she'd placed Delaney in his spot. Especially with the power of the law he wielded firmly behind him.

He hadn't deserved it. He'd been trying to warn her, to keep her on the straight and narrow. To be good for the rest of her life. He hadn't meant to terrify her. Okay, maybe he had, but not to panic her.

Not to have her question everything she did in light of his warning. But she had.

If he hadn't warned her, what would she have done differently? She'd still be afraid that she was too much like her own father. She'd still be worried that she wouldn't be a good parent. The conflict over not being able to have children would remain.

As if he heard the mess in her head, Constable Delaney said to Jenna, "She'd been badly hurt for years. But a month or two prior to the final blow, she'd been hospitalized with internal injuries."

Those memories washed through her. The pain. The shock. The dismay at learning she'd never have children.

The conversation still threaded through the air around them, and she knew she had to finish this. Gathering up her courage, she stepped back from Weaver's arms and turned to face the cop. Her hand entwined with Weaver's, a reassuring contact that she wasn't alone.

"I don't blame you for what you said that day." Her tone was harsher than she wanted it to be. Her words sharper.

With a sigh, she tried again. "I was so traumatized back then that your words just added to the rest of the nightmare in my life," she said. "I survived that childhood by learning to hold everything inside. So on the outside I looked calm and in control, cold even, whereas on the inside I was waiting for my world to blow up." She paused, adding, "I knew I'd done something horribly wrong in the eyes of society, so even though everyone at the time said I'd done what I needed to do and wouldn't be charged, I couldn't believe them. Your words aligned closer to the fears inside and meant you were more likely to be right than the others."

Weaver squeezed her hand. She smiled, staring down at their linked fingers, "So your words were the ones I remembered the most."

Delaney nodded. "It was that calm that worried me." He waited then added, "And I'm sorry for adding to your pain back then. You'd been through enough already. If I had a chance to do it all over again, I'd have approached the case very differently," he said, his tone apologetic yet sincere. "You've been on my mind since. I worried about you. When I saw you here…well, I'd hoped to clear the air."

For the first time, a natural smile crossed her lips. "And you did. Thank you for being persistent enough to push this. I wouldn't have done it without that." She slid a sideways look at Weaver. "I caught sight of you and Weaver speaking together this morning. I got quite a jolt."

She felt Weaver start, and then he squeezed her hand again.

"Has he been plotting this meeting then?" she asked.

"No," Delaney said. "I'd been trying to convince him to talk you into seeing me." The older man smiled. "He refused to do anything out of your comfort zone and wouldn't do anything to hurt you. He's been very protective."

"But I did know they'd be here tonight," Weaver said heavily. "I'm sorry, but this was something you had to do. An opportunity to deal with a huge issue."

She nodded absently, remembering the sadness in his voice, the sense of finality she remembered. As if the workshop was coming to an end, and so was their relationship.

Maybe it was at that. She was confused and overwhelmed, as if her past had been rewritten. But along with that crazy array of emotions was a lot of confusion over her feelings for him and his involvement.

Last night was too special. Today's ups and downs — traumatic.

So much had happened in such a short time she didn't know what she should feel no matter what she *did* feel. And could she trust any of it given the tumultuous events?

"As much as I don't appreciate the collaborative effort — I do appreciate it," she said quietly. "I wasn't strong enough to get here on my own."

"I didn't want to deceive you."

"But you had to." She nodded. "Got it."

But she dropped his hand, unable to reconcile the issue. She stared down at the floor, confusion and heartache twisting her up inside. Was it a good thing what he'd done? It was time to let this all go. But could she? Was it a betrayal? Yes. Did she want to forgive him? Hell yes. Could she? She had no idea.

The whole mess was exhausting. From the bad day, now the evening. She'd planned on dinner with Weaver and spending the night with him but had no idea where all of this left her. Left them.

Did he want to move forward, or was this over for him? Was this his goodbye? Not that it made any sense, but then nothing did right now.

Glancing over at Jenna, she saw her conversing quietly with Delaney. Paris didn't know if she was supposed to stay for her session tonight or if this was it. She hoped it was done – as in she was too tired for more analyzing. Especially her own psyche.

She needed to leave.

She needed to sort out the confusion going on.

She needed…she didn't know what.

Then she saw exactly what she needed. She burst into tears and ran.

Into the arms of the man who stood in the doorway.

Sean.

WEAVER WATCHED PARIS bolt and throw herself into the arms of a stranger.

Or maybe not. The two looked close enough to be family. And he knew. This was her brother Sean. The one whose life she saved.

He studied the man carefully, but all he really needed to see was the naked love in his face. This man cared about Paris like Weaver hadn't ever seen anyone care before.

Weaver's childhood had been shitty. But for these two, well, there were no words.

They'd been close during the abuse trying to help each other, and now that bond was even stronger today. He didn't know if Sean had come on his own or if he'd been called. For Paris's case, it was a good thing. But it also reminded him of his role in this. She'd turned away from him.

She'd gone running to Sean.

She didn't know or trust him.

She trusted and loved her brother.

He wasn't jealous of the bond between the siblings. But he'd love to be inside that inner circle. Unfortunately, the bond between family members, in this case brothers and sisters, often wasn't elastic enough to let others inside. This insight into the family unit hurt. It made him feel like a kid again when he hadn't belonged anywhere. Not even with his wife. She'd gone back to her family and left him behind. Now here, again, he was on the outside looking in.

Not that there wasn't room for him in the circle. But as yet, he hadn't been invited in.

Then he watched Paris take a step back, her face streaming with tears but smiling and laughing. She opened her arms to a woman standing just to the side. A woman whose face was badly disfigured, but her smile was stunning, showing the beauty within. From Paris's conversation, he realized this must be Robin. The woman Sean had met here at the seminar.

If there was a way to leave quietly, he'd slip out and go to his room. Leave Paris her privacy. Something he'd like right now, but there was no way to escape.

He felt disconnected. Uncomfortable. Unsure. Watching the tableau in front of him, he settled into a wider stance, crossed his arms, and waited.

CHAPTER 35

PARIS'S HEART SWELLED to bursting and then washed clean. A river of emotions flowed through her. So much pain. So much heartache. So much fear and so much love. For Weaver for making her do this. For Jenna who'd helped make this happen. For Sean who'd shown up to help her. She didn't know if he'd been called in to help her or if he'd instinctively known she was struggling to the point of no return.

And then there was Robin. That she'd come to support her was huge.

She had no idea how they'd been able to get in, but she was damn grateful they were here. Even more grateful that she could say, "I'm okay."

Sean, his hands clamped on her shoulders, held her back slightly so he could look into her eyes. Whatever he saw there made him smile. He tugged her closer and hugged her hard. "I'm very glad to hear that."

"Did you come down to try and talk me into seeing Delaney?"

Sean nodded. "Absolutely. This was *the* biggie in your world, and I would have done anything to help you get past it."

She wiped the tears from her eyes, gulping in fresh air. "Thank you."

"Don't thank me," he said easily. "I can't ever thank you enough for what you did."

"No thanks necessary." Smiling up mistily at her brother, she hugged him close. "I'm just sorry I didn't do it before he beat you so badly."

Sean shook his head. "It's over. We need to move on. We're good at that."

His gaze lifted and he surveyed the few people in the room. She could tell who he was looking at by the way his gaze changed. It softened when he came to Jenna, hardened when he glanced at Delaney, and widened when his all-too-perceptive gaze landed on Weaver.

Sean slanted a questioning gaze at her.

And damn if she didn't blush.

His grin was wide enough to split his face. "Jenna's magic maybe?"

"Maybe," she muttered in a low voice. "But maybe not. He was part of this."

"Good. I like him already."

She gasped and slapped him lightly. "That's not fair."

"Doing what needs to be done regardless of the personal cost to him is huge. And don't kid yourself about a huge personal cost in this case because there was – still is from the look on his face. As if he'd like to be a million miles away."

She stiffened and turned to face Weaver, but he was staring at Jenna and Delaney, an odd look on his face.

And she realized Sean was right. If he cared…he'd taken a huge risk of losing her if it ended up that his actions were so big she couldn't get over it.

"It's the betrayal," she murmured to her brother. "Aren't you supposed to support someone by not turning them in?"

"Unless turning them in is the only way for them to

move forward. In this case, you weren't going to see Delaney on your own. You needed to do this," he said seriously. "And doing what needs to be done is painful, and it's also painful for those around you."

"It could have backfired on him," she said, studying the cold detached look on his face.

"It did backfire on him."

She spun to look at her brother. "Why do you say that?"

"Because he's standing over there all alone. You're here with me, wondering what to do about him."

"I'm just still in shock… confused maybe," she protested, "I guess. I don't know. So much stuff has just happened that he's mixed up in that mess in my mind."

"Then separate him from that. He did what you weren't strong enough to do. That is worth so much. And if he's here, he's got his own problems and you're going to be triggering those."

Shit. She flinched, remembering his ex-wife who'd decided he was part of her past and she'd grown past him. Paris had just *done* something similar.

Her brother spoke quietly to her. "Now that I know you're going to be okay, I'm taking Robin out for dinner. Go talk to him."

She stepped forward and hugged him. "Thank you," she whispered. With a misty smile, she reached up and kissed him on the cheek then stepped back. "Best brother ever."

"Then go deal with the next problem."

Robin grinned at his side. "Then bring him for dinner on Sunday. We'd love to meet him."

Paris's gaze widened over the easy acceptance on their part. And she realized there was no guarantee about this outcome. "We'll see if I can fix this."

Sean's smile was breathtakingly full of love. "You can fix this. If you want to. You already know you'll do anything to save someone you love."

He took Robin's hand in his and with a gentle smile, they turned and walked out.

Delaney stepped forward and held out his hand. "You've become a beautiful woman inside and out. You always had that potential, but now you've grown into that promise. Congratulations, and I'm so sorry for my part that hurt you, scared you, or caused you any discomfort since we met." He shook her hand, gave her a sad smile, and walked out.

Now she had to face Jenna.

"Did you call Sean?" she asked Jenna.

"No." Jenna shook her head. "He's always known when you needed him. The same as you knew when he needed you, didn't you?"

Surprised, Paris thought back to that fateful day when she'd come running to her brother's aid. "I hadn't thought of it that way."

"Well, it is that way, and the good thing is you didn't need him this time. By the time he understood you were in trouble and the time it took for him to get here, you'd dealt with it." Her lips curled into a delighted smile. "I'm proud of you."

Paris started. "I'm not proud of me. I should have done this a long time ago," she muttered.

Jenna's beautiful laugh rang free. "Hindsight is always a gift. You weren't capable of doing anything about it before. You are now."

"And thanks for that."

"You owe Weaver thanks for that, too." She reached out a hand and clasped Paris on the shoulder. "We'd asked him earlier to help you and he refused. He didn't think you were ready and didn't want to do anything to hurt you."

Paris stared at her numbly. "He did?"

"He did. Today he knew you were running out of time, and he refused to do anything other than ask you to come – it was his condition that you be allowed to leave if you still weren't ready." Jenna stepped to the side. "So keep that in mind when you go to speak to him."

Paris was still standing in shock and dismay as Jenna walked around her and left the room. Paris spun around to face Weaver, wondering what to say. What could she say?

Only to realize she was alone. He'd already walked out.

WEAVER TOOK THE opportunity when she was busy talking to Delaney to slip away. He'd been walked out on before – not nice. There was no way he would stay there and wait for Paris's rejection. The awkward explanations. Difficult good byes. Been there and done that. What was that lesson he'd not learned? Oh yeah, don't fall for women who were in therapy.

Too bad he couldn't seem to remember that lesson before he got involved.

Pissed and hurt and afraid to look at his future, he made his way out the door and just kept walking. For hours. He needed to give her time. Anything less wasn't fair. But he didn't have to like it. Neither did he want to say goodbye.

He'd let her off easy. There had been enough heartache and trouble in her life already. Hell, she'd probably already let him go.

It was the way of healing. She'd moved on now.

Except they still had tomorrow to get through.

Tonight was a write off. Glancing at this watch, he was not surprised to see it was after nine already. He wished it were after midnight. Then he could go to bed. Not that he'd sleep. There was no way to get the thoughts of her out of his mind.

He'd hurt her.

There was no way around that. She'd consider it a betrayal. It wasn't. He'd done it because he cared about her. Knew she had to take this step. Felt like he had no choice if they wanted a future together. But damn, that was arrogant of him. It was her life. She had a right to take the steps she needed to take on her own time. In her own way.

He'd overstepped his boundaries. He'd been worried about that. That she'd blame him. But Jenna had convinced him otherwise. Still, he'd made sure she had the choice.

Only really – what choice did she have?

When there in the room, cornered by everyone – had she had a choice? Yes. But not much of one. And not an easy one to exercise. She'd not had access to the doorway to be able to leave, Jenna and Delaney had filled it.

Paris had to face them.

So she'd been coerced.

And he'd been a part of it.

Not liking himself very much at the moment, he sat dry-eyed on the same bench they'd sat on earlier today as the wind picked up around him. Leaving him cold – inside and out.

He had to trust she'd see his point of view. Believe in him. Believe in what they had.

Because really – given the choice – he'd do it all over again.

Because she was special.

He was… less so.

He'd learned more than he thought possible about himself – and her – during this workshop. Arriving with a pompous attitude and superior sense of self, he'd thought he was comfortable here at this place in his life. After all, he'd already done a ton of work on himself. To a certain point he was. But this workshop had shown him that he had further to go than he'd thought. Some of those steps he'd taken unknowingly.

Some of them lay before him.

He'd always felt unloved. That was his childhood speaking again. Memories rippled through his mind…maybe if his father had cared more for his son than that damn car, he wouldn't have gotten himself killed. If he'd been more lovable, then his mother would have preferred him to her bottle. Then there was his wife. She'd obviously not loved him either. Not if he had been a stepping stone to what she'd really wanted in life.

Up until now, he hadn't realized how much he'd tried to keep people at a distance so he wouldn't get hurt if they rejected him. He could have walked over to Paris's brother and introduced himself. Instead…he'd been the one to walk away. Escape rather than face them.

Like a little boy who had been rejected so many times, he was hell bent on rejecting everyone else first so he didn't have to deal with the pain again. He hadn't given them a chance to love him because he'd already assumed they wouldn't.

Hadn't he grown up at all? Why was he still giving that little boy so much credit for who he was now? Especially when he'd thought he'd walked away from that type of behavior a long time ago.

And what the hell was he going to do about it now?

CHAPTER 36

P ARIS SHIFTED HER position. The hallway floor was damn uncomfortable. She'd been waiting for hours. Her coffee cup was long empty. Then again, so was the one she brought for Weaver. It was after midnight and there was no sign of him.

She didn't know what to think. Had he left the workshop? Gone somewhere else for the night? If so – where? And was he coming back?

This couldn't end like this. She owed him an apology and if she were honest – a thank you. Sure it had been a shock and a tough thing to wrap her mind around, but now that she was on the other side of the meeting, she was emotionally drained but in a good way. It was a good thing he had done for her. But then he was going into the same profession as Jenna, so it made sense that he would.

Now that she'd gotten over her shock and come to understand, she wanted to be adult about all of this. But it wasn't going to happen if she couldn't connect with him. They still had to do a stupid project. And she had no idea what to do about that. She'd been hoping he'd have a miracle tucked up his sleeve that would save both their asses.

At this point, she was so exhausted, she figured she'd tell Jenna that she'd come up blank and had no project to hand in. What could Jenna do after all?

The hard floor woke her first. And movement. She groaned as she straightened, slowly getting to her feet.

And realized she wasn't alone.

Weaver stood frowning down at her.

She swayed. He grabbed her, holding her upright.

"Sorry, didn't mean to fall asleep," she whispered. "So tired."

"Shh." He unlocked his door and pushed the door open. "You should be in bed."

She closed her eyes and tried to open them again when the world went spinning out of control. She was lifted and carried into the bedroom, briefly put back on her feet, then laid down on the cool sheets.

"Need to talk," she murmured, shivering.

A blanket was tossed over her shoulders, and Weaver's deep voice said, "Sleep. We'll talk in the morning."

She slept.

With a smile on her face.

WEAVER STARED DOWN at her with mixed emotions. In the beginning, he'd tried to detach and had given that up early on when he realized he was already involved. Opening up to caring was painful. With her here in his bed, their future unsure – it was even more painful. "What the hell am I going to do with you," he murmured.

"Love me," she answered, but the words were so faint, her voice so low he thought he dreamt it. Wishful thinking on his part.

"I got that part covered," he whispered, his heart over-flowing with emotions.

There were huge black circles under her eyes, and even

under the blankets he could see the shivers making her thin frame shake. With a muttered curse, he quickly undressed and got in on the other side. She immediately rolled over and cuddled close.

As dawn crept forward, he realized he'd have to wake early and be ready for that talk they desperately needed to have.

They should have done it tonight – earlier. He'd do it now, but emotions were still hot and they were both exhausted. He doubted he could wake her enough to be cognizant at this point. No, risky as it was, he'd hold her close to his heart all night and hope that they could work through this in the morning.

He had a lot to think about. A lot of himself to assess. She'd done so much. Achieved so much. She'd shown him how to step up. He wasn't proud of his own actions. His own thoughts. But he knew he could change. Do what needed to be done to move forward. He wasn't a little kid anymore. It was time to leave all that hurt behind. Sure, it would rear up from time to time, but he didn't have to let the pain and fear control him.

Not any longer.

As he thought about the workshop and all he'd been through, both as an attendee and an observer, he thought again about the paper he'd planned to write.

Paris was right. He should do it.

But not about her. Not about the others.

But about him. She was right about that too. His experiences. His personal journey. His personal transformation.

Because that's what this week had been all about. He needed to let the image of who he was fall away, acknowledging that the hurt little boy still lived inside but no longer allowing him to rule his adult self.

And let his authentic self step forward.

What he had found with Paris was unique.

He'd do whatever he could to keep her in his life.

What they had together… it was so worth fighting for.

CHAPTER 37

PARIS WOKE SLOWLY. Heat from a furnace blasted all around her. It felt deliciously wonderful. She sighed and shifted, wincing at something digging into her side. Her bra strap?

She came aware in an instant. She lay in the unfamiliar room long enough to reorient herself and realize that Weaver slept beside her, his arm around her waist even now keeping her close, protecting her.

Again.

She hadn't done anything for him.

How sad. Relationships were supposed to be partnerships. She hadn't contributed anything.

Shifting, she groaned as the waistband of her pants tugged at her skin. Her dry, irritated skin. Shower time. She felt like crap, her eyelids heavy and caked with sleep. She slipped out of the bed and winced. Sleeping in clothes sucked.

Her shoes were on the floor by the bed. Quietly, she put them on and snuck her way to the door. This was not how she wanted him to see her. She looked and felt disgusting.

With a last glance, she realized he was sleeping heavily. She was instantly jealous. She'd tossed and turned all night.

Back in her room, she stripped and stepped under the hot running water, groaning in joy as her sore aching body eased back and her tender flesh shifted and moved freely. After a long soak and several washes of her hair, she turned off the water, better prepared to start the day.

Inside, she still felt like someone had reefed her insides out, put them under a microscope for a closer look, then stuffed them back in again.

Yesterday's session had been brutal. Last night's session…well, there weren't words.

But it was over.

And she'd survived.

Now to make it through today and she'd be good. This workshop had been intensive, deadly, and so worthwhile, but she wanted one more thing from it.

She wanted Weaver.

They needed to talk. If they had talked last night, it would have been better. Instead, he'd disappeared and she'd been exhausted – inside and out – and after searching, had parked herself outside his door waiting for him to come back. She'd wanted to spend the night with him – and she had, but not the way she intended.

It was also lousy to go to bed with her clothes on and wake up the same way.

Dressed, she checked the time. He needed to be woken up to get downstairs in time for the morning. If he cared to go. She also had to check out of the hotel. Did he? She packed up quickly and grabbed her card key. She'd leave her bag at the front desk while in the morning session.

Outside at the hallway, she walked across and knocked on Weaver's doorway. No answer.

"Weaver? We're late. Time to get moving."

No answer. Damn.

She picked up her bag and walked to the elevator. Maybe she could call him from the front desk. After she finished paying for her hotel room and left her bag with them, she tried to call his room and got no answer.

Not sure what else to do, she walked to the restaurant and grabbed two coffees and two muffins for the last time, carrying them to the conference room.

There were a few people working hard on filling out the last of the worksheets, ones she hadn't done either. The others worked on their projects. Something else she hadn't done. A hell of a morning.

Setting her load down, she grabbed her homework, quickly finished the first sheet, then came to her original ripped up, folded up mess of a sheet from the first day here.

The one she'd written on about killing her father.

And realized how far she'd come. The dreams she'd now be able to create and the pain she'd released.

Reading through the questions on her worksheet, she grinned. This one she might be able to do something with.

She quickly filled in the blanks and finished that part of her homework.

Then she pulled out her sheet with notes on the project. There was essentially nothing there. No instructions. Just something visual.

She sighed. Great. She could sing a song, do a dance, and draw little stick figures. Anything else? Hell no.

As she sat there frowning at the last assignment and in truth the biggest one, she was at a loss. She had no idea what to do.

All she could do was tell Jenna.

As she pondered the effects of actually not doing something for once, of failing…Jenna walked in. And Paris's stomach knotted.

Her mind whispered through all the past conditioning of failing, and she realized that it no longer mattered. Sure, failing and doing something wrong might give her some grief depending on the situation, but it wasn't going to get her a beating. Jenna might not be happy with her, but she wasn't going to hurt her over it.

In fact…

She might actually be fine with it.

Feeling lighter and easier and happier than she had been in a long time, she took a sip of coffee and realized the second cup of coffee was missing. Somehow, Weaver had slipped into his place beside her without her noticing.

Her whole body lit up. She smiled up at him. "Hey," she whispered, "I didn't see you come in."

His gaze was steady and searching. "You were deep in contemplation mode."

"Yeah, a lot of that going on this morning."

"And how are you?"

"Fine." She straightened, wanting to break down the strangeness between them. "Actually better than fine. I feel good. Younger. Freer."

"Good. That's the way it's supposed to be."

Jenna spoke up then, taking the attention off them and back to the program. They'd be given an hour to finish up their projects as several were done already and she'd be speaking with them at the back. Mid-morning, she had guest speakers coming in to talk to the group. There'd be a final lecture and time for questions, then they were free to go.

"What the hell are we going to do about this project?" she muttered. "I'm of half a mind to not do it."

He laughed. "I hear you. But I think that it's supposed to be an important step for our growth."

"Great, another one. So not. So, suggestions." She gave him a wry look. "We have less than an hour."

He grinned. "I do. It's more me doing something."

"Hey, I'm good with that," she joked.

"Okay, so let's ask you. I need a sheet of paper that has some of the toughest things written down on it. Something that you wish you didn't have to write, but they are honest and true and painful."

"Like Jenna's lovely worksheets?"

"Sure, that would be perfect."

She dug into her class assignments and pulled out three that had been ugly to do. "Will these work?" she asked.

"Yes, and this one…" he snagged up the ripped up sheet. "I gather the thing you wished you'd never done and ripped out of here was killing your father."

She sighed and nodded.

"Good." He stood up. "Have your coffee. I got this."

And he took her worksheets and walked out of the room.

She watched him leave until he turned down the hallway. She didn't have a clue what to do now. Normally she was the one who did everything. Even double-checking that everything was done correctly. Instead, this time she sat there and let him do everything.

As she sat, she realized *she* had transformed in the last five days. Even if Weaver was doing the final project for them both, Paris felt she should do something too. But nothing came to mind. No, Jenna had said *visual.* How the hell did a non-artistic person do something visual? Maybe she'd actually fail this part of the workshop.

She didn't have a picture of Delaney anywhere that she could use right now but if she had, she'd glue Weaver's face over the top.

Although that was an insult to Weaver.

Instead of making her cringe, she was okay with that. So maybe with this project she wasn't going to do well. That was all right too. She'd already done phenomenally well.

She'd have to take what she could get. Besides, she was well satisfied with her progress. Delighted actually.

An hour passed.

And another half an hour. No Weaver, and so far Paris hadn't been called to the back.

Good thing.

Then Jenna walked toward her. "Paris and Weaver – your turn."

Paris stood up and walked to the far corner where Jenna had set up a space for the projects. She took a glance around the room. No Weaver.

Okay, here it went. She took a deep breath and said, "I didn't do the final project."

Jenna's gaze widened, but not in shock. Surprise and then…joy shone in that gaze. As if Paris had done something wonderful.

She motioned for Paris to sit. "Now tell me how you feel."

"Like I didn't do what I was supposed to do," she confessed. "I don't feel like I failed, but that I should have tried harder."

"And when were you going to do that?" Jenna joked. "You've been through a lot lately."

"True, and honestly I owe my transformation to Weaver," she said. "He's been working on me since the beginning of the week. I know about the paper that he set aside for me. It caused me a lot of trouble at the beginning, but then I forgot about it. He was there when I needed him and often when I didn't. He didn't let me wallow or hide away even when I wanted to."

She gazed down at the files sitting in front of Jenna on the table. Hers and Weaver's folders both with photos clipped to the top. An idea came to her.

Someone called to Jenna. She stood up and excused herself for a moment and walked across the room.

Perfect.

Paris grinned, leaned forward, and snagged up both photos. Grabbing a pair of scissors sitting in a container with pens, she quickly cut what she'd wanted to and with the glue stick found in the same container, she glued the cut pieces together. Feeling like a kid in primary school but having fun anyway, she quickly created her visual.

There.

"Weaver…" Jenna said from behind her. "There you are."

"Sorry, it took me a little longer to do this right."

Paris looked up and gasped. "Oh my."

Weaver had created dozens of tiny origami birds from her worksheets and tied a fine string – dental floss, maybe, to each one. They hung from several coffee cups glued together as a hanging mobile.

"That is…beautiful." And it was. Delicate, imaginative, and so very appropriate.

"Stupid," he said. "But the theme was transformation. So I took her worksheets. The ones she'd worked hard on, cried tears over, and generally worked her ass off to do and transformed them to the wishes and dreams she'd hoped for and was working toward. Created these tiny birds to remind her of those dreams and all the hard work she'd put in to get here…and that she had the ability to make them take off and be something."

Paris barely heard, her eyes glued on the brilliant art piece.

The birds were tiny, maybe an inch across and created from folded paper done so well that she had a hard time seeing the details until she looked closer. He'd written little words on their wings. Children. Family. Freedom.

She sat back, stunned.

"That is amazing." She laughed, tears forming in the corner of her eyes. "And the best use of those damn worksheets I'd ever seen."

Jenna looked pained. "Hey, I worked hard to create those for you guys."

"And you did a great job. They are intensive, deep, and painful. But this…" Paris put her hand to her breast. "This is the best thing ever."

Impulsively, Paris jumped up and threw her arms around Weaver and kissed him. "Thank you."

With his free arm, he hugged her close. "Don't thank me. You lived this transformation." He gave the art piece a little shake. "But I watched it happen. So it was very visual for me."

Misty-eyed, she pulled him close. "Thanks. For being here all week. It was a tough time."

"But you got through it," he said firmly, "and you are in a much better place now."

She nodded, but sensing a distancing from him, she tightened her grasp and looked him in the eye. "True. And I couldn't have done it without you." At his head shake, she grinned. "Sure, I *might* have done this without you, but I'm glad I didn't have to. I'm glad you were there and that you stood by me. I know I put you in a tough spot, and so did Jenna and Delaney. I understand that you're afraid I'm like

your ex-wife and will walk away when I grow past this issue."
At his widening gaze, she shook her head and said, "But you're wrong. I know what I want. I always have. I know how to get it most times, too."

She paused, remembered what she had in her hands, and chuckled. "And just in case you thought that I am making this up, maybe you should see the corny amateur project I was about to hand over."

"What?"

She handed him her project – upside down.

He glanced over at Jenna, who shrugged her shoulders as she hadn't seen it yet, then slowly turned it over.

She'd taken both photos and glued them together and cut as they were, they were in the shape of a heart, both halves mostly complete but overlapping in a way that made them one.

"See," she whispered, "You're not in this alone. I'm here too."

And she reached up and clasped his hand that held the photos.

He gazed at the photos, his throat moving, then slowly lifted his gaze to her. The moist brightness in them made her heart squeeze tight. He went to say something, only he couldn't get the words out.

Snatching her up into his arms, he buried his head in her hair.

"You win," he whispered. "Your project is the best."

"No," she whispered right back. "We both win. Because we found each other."

And she pulled back to look up at him, adding, "Thank heavens."

And with the photo crushed between them, he lowered his head and kissed her.

Author's Note

Thank you for reading Scales! If you enjoyed the book, please take a moment and leave a short review.

Dear reader,

I love to hear from readers, and you can contact me at my website: www.dalemayer.com or at my Facebook author page. To be informed of new releases and special offers, sign up for my newsletter or follow me on BookBub. And if you are interested in joining Dale Mayer's Reader Group, here is the Facebook sign up page.
http://geni.us/DaleMayerFBGroup

Cheers,
Dale Mayer

Previews

Second Chances

Go ahead. Take Charge of your life. Move forward…if you can…

Changing her future means letting go of her past. Karina heads to a weekend seminar and discovers the speaker is the person she needs to move on from. But she soon realizes bigger issues are facing her…

Brian has moved on, at least he'd believed he had… until he sees Karina in his audience…and realizes he's been lying to himself.

Passion pulls them together, love binds them together, but a revengeful enemy determines to keep the two apart…and destroy them both.

Second Chances Sample

Chapter 1

HER HEART RACING, Karina pushed open the glass double doors and walked into the almost deserted pub. Her breath quickened as she searched the faces of the few patrons inside. *Had he left already?* Or was Brian Saunders somewhere here, drowning his sorrows? Wendy, Brian's girlfriend of two years, had broken up with him and taken off for Europe, or some such thing. Karina knew she should feel sorry for him, but instead her mind wouldn't stop pestering her.

Here's your chance. One last shot to make him notice you before you go home and never see him again.

That the timing sucked wouldn't stop her.

Besides, if anyone asked, she was just here having a drink. And she could use one. Her last exam was done. She'd finally finished school and damn if she didn't feel like crying instead of cheering.

"Hey, Karina, thought you'd have booked it by now."

She waved at one of several friends having a good time at a nearby table. Most of the students who'd finished exams had already left, and the few stragglers writing tomorrow were either cramming or here trying to forget about writing in the morning.

"Nah. Leaving in the morning. It's a long drive and I *so* don't want to deal with that tonight. Or the ferry."

That elicited several nods. Anyone who lived on Vancouver Island knew about ferry woes to the mainland. She'd tossed around the idea of staying on the island, had even looked for work, but nothing had come of it, so she was heading home to Vancouver. Victoria, and the university in particular, would stay a happy memory. And, in some ways, a tough one.

She ordered a draft at the bar and turned around to take another look. Maybe she'd missed Brian in her first skim.

Shit. Ian Blackburn was here, too. And he'd seen her. Shit, shit, and triple shit. He'd always been super friendly to her, but there was something about him that gave her the creeps. And then last week she'd seen another side of him altogether. A professor in one of the classes they'd been in together had given Ian a poor grade on an assignment. Ian had lost it…big time. Someone had even called campus security to get him out of the lecture hall. He'd turned into something that terrified her and probably every other student there. She shuddered at the memory.

Karina turned around and glanced the other way, deliberately putting her back to Ian.

And there he was. *Brian.*

Her heart sighed even as it started to pound. She should go over to him. He looked sad, like he'd lost his best friend. Which, after the end of a two-year relationship, she guessed he had. But Karina told herself she was still a friend, right? Albeit a casual one, but still… They'd had classes together, the odd beer-and-pizza night as part of a group. That kind of thing. He had no idea that she'd been in love with him for a long time. She'd been careful to keep her feelings hidden. He

hadn't been free and she wasn't the type to break up relationships.

She checked out the other half of the bar before her gaze
zinged back to Brian. He lifted his beer bottle and poured
the remaining golden liquid down his throat. Slamming the
empty down, he reached for the spare, waiting. Damn, she
hated to see him like this.

All right. She was going to go over there. Just a sip of
beer for courage, first. She raised her glass to her lips.

"Karina. I'm glad you're here. I was hoping to see you
before you left. May I sit?"

Ian. Shit. He'd somehow evaded her awareness and seated himself on the barstool next to her without her knowing.
This was what she got for being nice and polite to a guy who
mistook it for encouragement and, frankly, gave her the
willies.

She attempted a smile behind her glass as she drowned a
big gulp. She had to get away. Now.

"Sorry, I came here to meet someone." She said it lightly, dismissively. She'd planned to wait another minute or two
before approaching Brian, but Ian's crowding was forcing her
hand. "Oh, there he is. Brian."

She got up and waved in Brian's direction, tossing a
good-bye smile at Ian.

His brows came together in a dark vee and his lips
thinned, the expression causing her smile to falter and her
stomach to heave. His thick nose and heavy brows might
indicate a Mediterranean ancestry, but the darkness in his
eyes gave her the spooks.

"I hadn't realized."

Keeping her face averted she took another big step and
cast a glance back, relief washing over her when he didn't

follow, but instead walked back to his seat.

Well, she'd started down this road, so…

"Hey." She slapped a bright, friendly smile on her face and sat down across from Brian. Now that she was safely seated her unease over Ian abated, even while her heart lurched at the deep unhappiness on Brian's face.

He looked up at her, a lopsided attempt at a smile peeking out. "Hi, Karina. I'm not good company right now."

"Oh." She didn't know what to say. His pain was a palpable thing. Impulsively, she reached across the table and laid her hand on his. "I heard and I'm sorry."

Surprise lit the dark depths of his chocolate eyes.

When he didn't say anything, she stood. She'd intruded on his private pain, and that wasn't right. She turned to leave.

"Wait." His husky voice reached out to her. "Please, don't go."

She smiled warmly at him and sat back down.

She stayed there for several more rounds as they talked deep into the night. Once or twice she glanced over at Ian. Every time she looked he appeared to be seething with anger as he stared toward her and Brian. She shuddered.

"This place is closing soon." She tugged Brian to his feet. "Come on, you look ready to drop."

"I'm not that bad," he protested, but allowed himself to be shuffled out the door. The cool night air hit them and snapped some of the buzz away. Karina looked at the stars, her heart full and happy. Not exactly a dream date, but it was Brian…and her…alone.

"Let's go to my place. I think I have a bottle of wine," he suggested.

"You're going to fall asleep before you ever get it open,"

she scoffed as she fell into step beside him.

He looked at her, his little-boy expression pleading that it couldn't possibly be bedtime already. "I don't want to be alone tonight," he admitted softly. "Please come share a bottle of wine with me." There was only a slight slur to his voice and she'd had just enough to drink to feel the same.

Besides, she didn't want the night to end either. It might not be the wisest move but she couldn't come up with any convincing reasons why she shouldn't spend the last few hours with him.

She gave in.

He grinned at her, wrapping an arm around her shoulders. "How come we didn't do this before?" His sloppy grin made her heart laugh. "We should have. I've always liked you."

Magical words.

They walked toward his room, arms around each other, talking, murmuring in low voices. The heat of his voice, the tenor of his words, the glow of moonlight, Brian's touch – it was magic. And she wanted more. She wanted it all. To-night.

THE COUPLE WALKED down the path, sliding in and out of view. He'd hidden in the trees thinking to see where Brian was taking Karina. And hoping his instinctive guess was wrong.

But no; there she was. Ian thought he'd missed her leaving. But no, she'd left with Brian. Why? *Why Brian?* Brian was nothing. And he had a girlfriend. Or he'd had a girlfriend. According to the gossip, he'd just been dumped.

How could Karina do such a thing? It's not like Brian

was in any shape to enter another relationship right now. Had she no respect. For him? Or for herself?

He stood in the shadows of the trees that darkened the path and watched them make their way to Brian's dorm. Anger simmered inside.

Brian had many girls fawning all over him. He didn't need Karina. He'd only cast her off later.

Karina deserved better. If she weren't so blinded by Brian's flashy looks, she'd realize it. She'd be sorry later.

Damn Brian to hell.

SATISFACTION THRUMMED THROUGH Karina's body as she collapsed beside Brian in the wee hours of the morning. Her skin was damp and her body buzzed from their heated lovemaking. "Who'd have thought?" she whispered into the darkness.

A deep rumble rolled out from his chest as he attempted to speak but couldn't. She grinned. She'd brought him to this. She'd been the one he'd turned to tonight. Not Wendy, but her – Karina. Maybe she shouldn't have jumped at the opportunity…but she'd needed the chance to show him how good they could be together. How perfect.

And given that exams were over and all students going their separate ways, it had been now or never.

It seemed she'd loved him for so long. Always an acquaintance, never quite a friend and always superficial, kept on the outside…the last place she wanted to be.

She could no more stop blurting the words than she could stop the tidal wave of love that swept through her, giving the words their freedom.

"I love you," she whispered and dropped a kiss on his

bare chest, before nestling her head on his shoulder and falling asleep.

MORNING DAWNED BRIGHT and clear. Karina woke slowly, her body still warm and achy from the night's activities. She bolted upright as memories flooded back. *Brian.* She'd had the most wonderful night of her life. She grinned and bounded out of bed.

Wrapping herself in the sheet, she walked out to the communal room, grateful that Brian's roomies had already left. *Empty.* She stood in the middle of the room, dread forming a sinking ball of steel in her stomach. An engine started outside.

She raced over to the glass doors, stepping out onto the small verandah in time to see Brian's car disappearing down the drive at a good clip. *He was coming back, wasn't he?* She stood there, waiting, for a long time after his car disappeared from view. As her heart broke into a dozen tiny pieces, hope faded away. The small sedan was gone.

And he hadn't once looked back.

TO BE CONTINUED…

Touched by Death

Adult RS/thriller

Death had touched anthropologist Jade Hansen in Haiti once before, costing her an unborn child and perhaps her very sanity.

A year later, determined to face her own issues, she returns to Haiti with a mortuary team to recover the bodies of an American family from a mass grave. Visiting his brother after the quake, independent contractor Dane Carter puts his life on hold to help the sleepy town of Jacmel rebuild. But he finds it hard to like his brother's pregnant wife or her family. He wants to go home, until he meets Jade – and realizes what's missing in his own life. When the mortuary team begins work, it's as if malevolence has been released from the earth. Instead of laying her ghosts to rest, Jade finds herself confronting death and terror again.

And the man who unexpectedly awakens her heart – is right in the middle of it all.

This book is available. Sample chapter is next...

Touched by Death Sample

Prologue

IN PERFECT SYMPHONY the clouds swayed in the sky, wrapping the moon in protective cotton wool as the ground shook and trembled beneath the sleepy town of Jacmel in the south of Haiti.

Mother Earth growled and raged over and over again as if she knew the secrets long kept hidden in the hills behind the small town. As if she knew about the injustices done. As if she knew this had to stop. She gave one last mighty shove and the earth cracked open.

Trees toppled, their roots ripped from the ground in hapless destruction. Large rocks tumbled as their foundations were wiped out from below. Everything fell to the force of Mother Nature – at long last exposing old secrets to the light.

When she was finally satisfied, the clouds slipped back from their protective stance, letting the moon glare upon the result of Mother Earth's game of fifty-two pickup with the Devil. The rays shone on bones long picked clean – now newly exposed to the sky.

The ground undulated one last time. The surrounding hillside shuddered, sending a light dusting of earth and rock to rebury the gruesome evidence. As if the sins of man were too much for even the moon to see.

FIVE DAYS LATER, a tractor, hastily called into service, with a bucket on the front, groaned as it carried yet another load of the town's dead to a large grave. Herman, the tractor driver, was beyond pain and grief and death. He focused on the gritty details of plain survival. Five days of heat and exposure hadn't been kind to the dead – or to the living. Survival had become a grim business and rotting bodies needed to be buried or disease would crush them further. So many dead. No money. No time. No help.

No choice.

His neighbor, John, lifted the last small corpse from the dump truck load on the ground to the loader's bucket. He pulled off one work glove, straightened the bandana tied around his mouth and nose and shouted, "Good to go!"

Herman popped the gear shift forward, swore and prayed that Bertha would survive the job given her. He trundled forward. "Come on girl." He patted the stick shift in his hand. "I need you to get it done. If you quit on me, I ain't gonna make it through this." And that was no joke. He knew for damn sure that he wouldn't if ol' Bertha didn't. *Bad business this*. He had respect for the dead. Every one of his family and friends had received a proper send off, a decent burial – as was fitting. Until this earthquake.

Pain clutched his heart and squeezed. So many dead.

He'd lost his wife, one son and two grandkids this last week. Sex and age hadn't mattered here. Mother Nature hadn't cared. She'd wiped them all out.

John, the only other person who'd stepped up to help, had been lucky. His young wife and her family had survived the devastation. Living out of town had helped. That also contributed to his motivation to help out. This grave butted against his wife's family's land so it made sense for John to make sure this grave was closed over right and proper. There could be many people trekking to the grave on All Soul's Day, as families came to honor their dead. Then again, complete families had been buried together. There might not be anyone left to mourn.

He would come and visit. There were too many people here to forget.

Herman tugged at the old t-shirt tied around his nose and mouth, his black skin blending with the poor light. Nothing kept the smell out. He'd already gone through a half dozen pairs of gloves. But without the makeshift bandana the breath caught in his chest, making him gag. His clothes would have to be burned after this. There would be no way to clean them.

Bertha struggled forward. Darkness hid the evidence of what they were doing. What he'd done. He only hoped he wouldn't have too many more loads to haul.

In the aftermath of the earthquake, everyone had been numb, in shock or frozen with grief. No one had been able to make decisions. There'd been no army to take care of the problem. The government buildings and staff had been as decimated as the rest of the population.

Herman hadn't been able to leave his people lying exposed like that. Determined to do what he could he'd taken command and had done something. Something so awful, he couldn't close his eyes without seeing the stares of the dead – blaming him.

So far, close to sixty people had gone into this pit. The natural depression, a ready-made burial spot, was a godsend to the desperate survivors, a fast answer to the bloated dead rotting on the sidewalks. He didn't know how many more were to come, maybe hundreds. Later, much later, if someone cared, they could open this mass grave and do the right thing. But not now. Now they had to get on with the business of survival.

Mother Nature was a bitch.

Chapter 1

One year later...

JADE HANSEN TWISTED in the cool sheets. Her sweaty panicked body searched for a way out of the endless nightmare of bloated bodies, desperate people and cries for help – pleas that would never get answered. She turned in the fog as one more person, caught among the fallen rocks, cried out to her. She came face to face with a woman – blood congealed in her hair and streaked down the side of her face, a chunk of concrete crushing her legs. She begged for Jade to find her son.

Screaming, Jade took off to the safety of the tent, the tent filled with the dead...and the living that searched for their families.

She couldn't help them all.

She couldn't help any of them.

She couldn't even help herself.

With tears streaming down her face, Jade woke in a panic as if the demons of her nightmare had followed her into the present.

Shuddering, she recognized the hanging lamp overhead as the one in her apartment. The Aztec print couch she'd fallen asleep on was hers, a gift from her brother. And she finally understood that the evening's in-depth television coverage of a small earthquake in Haiti had been the trigger for her nightmare.

Jade curled into a ball, pulling her throw higher up on her neck. She winced at the images still flashing on the news. Another earthquake in Haiti. Only a little one this time. Not that the size mattered. The memories of her one and only humanitarian trip to that area, after the major earthquake almost a year ago, had etched themselves permanently into her brain. A horrible time, a-praying-on-your-knees-for-help kind of horrible time. In Haiti, nightmares had destroyed her sleep. The shortage of food for those suffering had destroyed her appetite.

She'd lost weight over there, but nothing compared to the pounds that had slipped off after her return home. Sure, that had been almost a year ago. It didn't matter. With the nightmare fresh in her mind it felt like only two days.

So much pain and suffering. *So much torment.* She couldn't stop it. She couldn't even begin to make it right. There'd been nothing she could do to help – or so little relative to the scope of the problem, it might as well have been nothing. If she'd been offered a ride out of that hell on any given day, she'd have jumped over her colleagues to grab it.

She wasn't proud of that.

In fact, it made her feel small and ashamed. Her colleagues had done so much better.

She'd wanted to be better. She'd tried to be better.

She'd failed. Failed her colleagues. The victims. And herself.

The memories still haunted her.

She had her nice safe lab job back in Seattle. She drove to work every day in a nice car and returned home every night to her clean safe apartment with running water, heat and electricity. All the comforts denied the Haitians still struggling through the devastation.

After she'd locked her front door behind her that first day home, the tears had started to pour. It seemed she'd been crying ever since.

Her life had gone from bad to worse for a while before she'd picked up – somewhat.

And now another earthquake.

If a small one like that triggered her memories what was the reality doing to all those poor people still living the horror?

The phone rang.

She ignored it.

It wouldn't quit. Finally, she couldn't stand it so picked up the receiver. She didn't even bother to check the caller ID. Duncan called every night at nine.

"I'm fine, Duncan."

"Hey, Kitten." Her brother's pet name for her made her smile as he'd probably intended. She used to be like him. Upbeat, funny and carefree. Until life had dumped her on her ass at the top of the slide and given her a hard kick downhill. She wasn't sure she'd hit bottom now either.

"I've got a job proposition for you."

His cheerful voice made her want to smile. The job proposition didn't. "I don't want to hear it."

He laughed, a buoyant sound that rang around the room. He never failed to raise her spirits. The effect just didn't hang around after his calls. "Maybe you don't, but maybe you do. How will you know if you don't hear it? It's a good one."

His wheedling tone made her smile in spite of her horrible mood. "Not if I don't want to hear it."

"You don't know what you want."

Jade groaned. "If I don't know, then how do you?"

That laughter pealed again. She shook her head and felt the lightness – the joyful spirit that was her brother – ease the ache in her soul. "I know you keep trying to save me, Duncan, but I'm fine."

The laughter and joy cut off suddenly. Duncan's voice, sober and sad, whispered, "No. No, you're not."

Tears choked her. She rubbed her eyes. She wasn't going to cry, damn it. Not tonight. Not *again* tonight.

"This has to stop, Jade. You're going to collapse and I don't want that to happen." Love slipped through the phone receiver making it harder to hold back the tears. Jade didn't trust herself to speak. She sniffled ever so slightly.

"I know you're hurting inside. I feel it and I hurt for you."

"I know," she whispered, starting to shake, knowing she had to stop – only she didn't know how. And once again – couldn't deal with it. "Look, I'm really tired. I need to get to bed. I'll talk to you tomorrow."

She didn't give him a chance to say good-bye and hung up instead. As soon as the receiver clicked down, the tears rolled. Hot and steady, they streamed down her cheeks. She snuggled back into the couch and let them run.

The point of stopping them was long gone – besides she no longer knew how.

"HEY DANE. THAT guy called again." John called out.

"Yeah, which guy?" Dane walked over to stand beside his stepbrother who'd stopped by the site for a visit.

Dane tugged his hard hat off to wipe the sweat running

down his forehead. Christ it was hot and humid here. He surveyed the hospital construction site in front of them. Not bad at all. They were ahead of schedule, but completion of the new wing was still months away. Jacmel hadn't recovered from the last big earthquake and with smaller ones continually causing setbacks, the country would be years getting back on its feet.

It had taken weeks to convince John to let him come over after the quake. When he'd realized how badly in need the town was, Dane had stepped in. But John had refused Dane's help to fix John's small engine repair shop that had been decimated in one of the smaller more recent earthquakes. John said he wanted to fix things himself.

"The guy about the grave." John said, "Remember they want to open it and retrieve some guy's family?"

Dane glanced over at his brother. There were only the two of them left in the family. Both stubborn. Independent. And family oriented. It had only taken one phone call with something odd in John's voice to catch Dane's attention. He'd put his Seattle construction business in the hands of his capable foreman, an old school friend, and without his brother's invite, he'd flown to Haiti two days later. That had been months ago.

Shielding his eyes from the hot sun, Dane said, "I have to admit, never-ending sunshine and warm, dry weather is hardly a hardship. Of course we haven't hit the humid summer season, yet."

"See? Isn't this much better than the wet misery of the coast? Seattle is probably still buried in snow – even in March." John grinned with satisfaction.

Dane couldn't argue that. His foreman had been complaining of just that in the last phone call. "Not everyone hates the rain like you do."

"Come on, admit it." John reached over and smacked Dane's shoulder. A cloud of dust rose, making him step back hurriedly. "You love it here."

"I love visiting you and of course, I adore Tasha." Dane grinned over his white lie. There was no arguing that Tasha obviously adored his brother so that was good enough for him. It had, after all, been the call of family that had brought Dane here.

John had a terrible history with relationships. His long-time high school sweetheart had walked out the door of her home one day just weeks before graduation and had never returned. A few years later, John had married the witchy Elise. That marriage had been a walking disaster right from the wedding reception. Dane hadn't been able to stand the woman and the feeling had been mutual. John was just a big teddy bear who attracted unscrupulous people.

After that fiasco, John disappeared for years before finally setting up housekeeping with Tasha in Haiti. Dane's antennae went off at that and given the past, he could be forgiven for worrying about his brother. Only John appeared to have stabilized, was flourishing even. Dane had been delighted.

The major earthquake had changed all that, sending John back into the same morose angry man as before.

"Hey, are you in there?"

Dane started.

John smirked at him, a sign his light-hearted kid brother was showing through the more cynical angry one of recent years. "What's the matter; Felice getting to you?"

Heat washed over Dane's throat. Felice was too hot, too willing and way too young. She was also the daughter of one of Tasha's friends who'd visited yesterday. He didn't know the specific laws in Haiti relating to that sort of thing, still he was pretty damn sure he'd get jail time back home and that was deterrent enough for him.

"She needs to be locked away for a few years."

"Not here. Girls her age are often married and pregnant." John added thoughtfully, "And not likely in that order."

Dane shook his head. "As long as it's not to me."

John changed the subject abruptly. "What am I going to do about the call…about this guy's request for help at the mass gravesite? Sounds crazy to me."

Easily following the lightning shift of his brother's mind, Dane said, "What's to do – he's a grieving man. His request isn't unreasonable. And it's done all the time."

John visibly shuddered. "I never expected to feel so strongly about it, but after that earthquake… I don't know Dane. I saw too much death. More than I should have – more than anyone should have. It seems wrong to dig up those poor earthquake victims again."

"You've been living here too long. Some weird Haitian's beliefs are rubbing off on you."

John snickered, making Dane laugh. "Or not long enough. According to Tasha, Mother Earth claimed them and she won't be happy if she's forced to give them up again."

With a sigh of disgust, Dane said, "That's crazy talk. This guy lost his family. He wants to take the three of them home to Seattle and bury them properly. He needs closure. That's all. What's so wrong about that?"

John kicked a stray rock in the dirt. "I don't know that anything is wrong with it. I guess if it were me and mine, I'd want to take them home, too. But it's a mass grave. There are other bodies to consider. Other families who will be hurt."

"Really?" Dane stared at him. "Like *how mass?*"

John shot him a look before grimacing and staring off in the horizon. "I stopped counting at sixty. We did what we had to do. The dead…they were everywhere. Herman, our old neighbor, used his loader…Christ it was bad."

Dane scrunched his face. John rushed to explain.

"God, there were children playing beside bloated bodies. They'd become dulled to them; there were so many. Oh don't blame the children. They stayed close to the people they knew because they had no one else. That a dead mother or sibling lay within a few feet didn't seem to matter. Even dead, they were a comfort."

Dane closed his eyes as terrible images flooded his mind. He couldn't imagine the horror. "I wasn't judging. I just can't envision what you went through. And to think of children sitting there, so lost and alone… Well…it's a terrible thought."

Shadows darkened John's eyes. Dane was sorry for what John had been through. "That's the thing about family." Dane patted John on the shoulder and noticed his brother cringe.

"So you think this guy should be allowed to come in and remove his kin?" John wasn't backing away from this one.

"I don't have any say in this. I wasn't aware that you did, either. I'm sure this man has already gone through the authorities. I'd suggest that you accept that this is going to happen whether you want it to or not. The team of special- ists is going to be here soon. When they arrive, be nice to them. Helpful. They will probably be there for a day or two, a week or two max. Then they'll be gone, leaving the others to rest in peace."

"It's not that easy."

"I know. There are other people with loved ones in that grave. Maybe someone should suggest that all the victims be identified and even..." Dane pursed his lips and nodded his head, pleased with his idea. "Reburied properly. This guy has money. Maybe some of it should be put toward assisting the community to help them deal with disaster."

John shook his head. "You don't understand the full scope of the problem here. There could be hundreds of bodies there. We just kept putting them in then piling dirt and rocks on top to make sure they weren't disturbed. We probably went overboard on that part."

Dane blanched. "Hundreds?" He swallowed heavily. "Okay so maybe the team will need a little longer. Still something could be done for the other remains." Dane winced. "Or at least the remains they can find and identify while they search for the ones they are shipping back to Seattle."

John stared at him, and gulped. "That's not helping."

"Yeah. I know. Sorry about that."

The two men stared at the half-completed building in front of them. Dane took an involuntary step back. Right now the damn thing resembled a skeleton reaching out of the ground.

TO BE CONTINUED...

Tuesday's Child

What she doesn't want…is exactly what he needs.

Shunned and ridiculed all her life for something she can't control, Samantha Blair hides her psychic abilities and lives on the fringes of society. Against her will, however, she's tapped into a killer – or rather, his victims. Each woman's murder, blow-by-blow, ravages her mind until their death releases her back to her body. Sam knows she must go to the authorities, but will the rugged, no-nonsense detective in charge of tracking down the killer believe her?

Detective Brandt Sutherland only trusts hard evidence, yet Sam's visions offer clues he needs to catch a killer. The more he learns about her incredible abilities, however, the clearer it becomes that Sam's visions have put her in the killer's line of fire. Now Brandt must save her from something he cannot see or understand…and risk losing his heart in the process.

As danger and desire collide, passion raises the stakes in a game Sam and Brandt don't dare lose.

Broken Protocols

Romantic comedy & suspense

Dani's been through a year of hell…

Just as it's getting better, she's tossed forward through time with her orange Persian cat, Charmin Marvin, clutched in her arms. They're dropped into a few centuries into the future. There's nothing she can do to stop it, and it's impossible to go back.

And then it gets worse…

A year of government regulation is easing, and Levi Blackburn is feeling back in control. If he can keep his reckless brother in check, everything will be perfect. But while he's been protecting Milo from the government, Milo's been busy working on a present for him…

The present is Dani, only she comes with a snarky cat who suddenly starts talking…and doesn't know when to shut up.

In an age where breaking protocols have severe consequences, things go wrong, putting them all in danger…

It's a Dog's Life

Romantic comedy & suspense

It's the first day of Ninna's job in the local animal shelter…and a dog is talking to her. Not just any dog…a fat, old, smart-alecky Basset Hound who says his name is Mosey.

She can't quit, she needs this job. And then there's the yummy vet. Who turns out to live across the street from her in a much bigger house than her tiny house. Big enough to hold a few animals – including the mouthy Mosey. With all this going on, she doesn't have time to worry about the rash of break-ins and the sense of being watched. She's too busy worrying that she's nuts.

When Ninna agrees to dog sit for the cute vet from work, she sees it as a trial at being a pet owner and a way to build on her budding relationship with the vet. For Mosey, this weekend means time to get to know each other.

For the stalker who's tracking Ninna's movements, it means…opportunity.

About the Author

Dale Mayer is a *USA Today* best-selling author, best known for her SEALs military romances, her Psychic Visions series, and her Lovely Lethal Garden cozy series. Her contemporary romances are raw and full of passion and emotion (Broken But ... Mending, Hathaway House series). Her thrillers will keep you guessing (Kate Morgan, By Death series), and her romantic comedies will keep you giggling (*It's a Dog's Life*, a stand-alone novella; and the Broken Protocols series, starring Charming Marvin, the cat).

Dale honors the stories that come to her—and some of them are crazy, break all the rules and cross multiple genres!

To go with her fiction, she also writes nonfiction in many different fields, with books available on résumé writing, companion gardening, and the US mortgage system. All her books are available in print and ebook format.

Connect with Dale Mayer Online

Dale's Website – www.dalemayer.com
Twitter – @DaleMayer
Facebook Page – geni.us/DaleMayerFBFanPage
Facebook Group – geni.us/DaleMayerFBGroup
BookBub – geni.us/DaleMayerBookbub
Instagram – geni.us/DaleMayerInstagram
Goodreads – geni.us/DaleMayerGoodreads
Newsletter – geni.us/DaleNews

Also by Dale Mayer

Published Adult Books:

Psychic Vision Series

Tuesday's Child

Hide'n Go Seek

Maddy's Floor

Garden of Sorrow

Knock, Knock…

Rare Find

Eyes to the Soul

Now You See Her

Shattered

Into the Abyss

Psychic Visions Books 1–3

Psychic Visions Books 4–6

Psychic Visions Books 7–9

By Death Series

Touched by Death – Part 1

Touched by Death – Part 2

Touched by Death – Parts 1&2

Haunted by Death

Chilled by Death

By Death Books 1–3

Second Chances...at Love Series

Second Chances – Part 1

Second Chances – Part 2

Second Chances – complete book (Parts 1 & 2)

Charmin Marvin Romantic Comedy Series

Broken Protocols

Broken Protocols 2

Broken Protocols 3

Broken Protocols 3.5

Broken Protocols 1-3

Broken and... Mending

Skin

Scars

Scales (of Justice)

Broken but... Mending 1-3

Glory

Genesis

Tori

Celeste

Glory Trilogy

Biker Blues

Biker Blues: Morgan, Part 1

Biker Blues: Morgan, Part 2

Biker Blues: Morgan, Part 3

Biker Baby Blues: Morgan, Part 4

Biker Blues: Morgan, Full Set

Biker Blues: Salvation, Part 1

Biker Blues: Salvation, Part 2

Biker Blues: Salvation, Part 3

Biker Blues: Salvation, Full Set

SEALs of Honor

Mason: SEALs of Honor, Book 1

Hawk: SEALs of Honor, Book 2

Dane: SEALs of Honor, Book 3

Swede: SEALs of Honor, Book 4

Shadow: SEALs of Honor, Book 5

Cooper: SEALs of Honor, Book 6

Markus: SEALs of Honor, Book 7

Evan: SEALs of Honor, Book 8

Mason's Wish: SEALs of Honor, Book 9

SEALs of Honor, Books 1–3

SEALs of Honor, Books 4–6

Collections

Dare to Be You…

Dare to Love…

Dare to be Strong…

RomanceX3

Standalone Novellas

It's a Dog's Life

Riana's Revenge

Published Young Adult Books:

Family Blood Ties Series

Vampire in Denial

Vampire in Distress

Vampire in Design

Vampire in Deceit

Vampire in Defiance

Vampire in Conflict

Vampire in Chaos

Vampire in Crisis

Vampire in Control

Vampire in Charge

Family Blood Ties Set 1–3

Family Blood Ties Set 1–5

Family Blood Ties Set 4–6

Family Blood Ties Set 7–9

Sian's Solution – A Family Blood Ties Short Story

Design series

Dangerous Designs

Deadly Designs

Darkest Designs

Design Series Trilogy

Standalone

In Cassie's Corner

Gem Stone (a Gemma Stone Mystery)

Time Thieves

Published Non-Fiction Books:

Career Essentials

Career Essentials: The Résumé

Career Essentials: The Cover Letter

Career Essentials: The Interview

Career Essentials: 3 in 1